KISSING
HER CRAZY

A CRAZY LOVE STORY

KIRA
ARCHER

Entangled Publishing, LLC
2614 South Timberline Road
Suite 109
Fort Collins, CO 80525
Visit our website at www.entangledpublishing.com.

Lovestruck is an imprint of Entangled Publishing, LLC.

Edited by Erin Molta and Heather Howland
Cover design by Heather Howland
Cover art from iStock

Manufactured in the United States of America

First Edition October 2015

To the hubs and my kidlets and all the exciting new chapters in our lives.

Chapter One

Elliot aimed his most enticing smile at the bikini-clad brunette who was making her third circuit past his chaise lounge. He was glad his sunglasses covered his eyes so he didn't have to put forth the effort to make the smile genuine. It wasn't that she wasn't completely hot. She was. And usually he'd be more than interested. But lately, he'd gotten a little tired of the bevy of girls only too willing to be seen on the arm of Elliot Debusshere.

That realization surprised him a bit. He'd always enjoyed the perks that came with being the only son of two very successful parents. His sisters had been much more sheltered. Controlled. One had taken to it better than the other. Lilah was, and continued to be, their mother's perfect little angel. Only his twin Cherice had had the courage and drive to get out on her own. Do what she wanted. Be happy. He envied her.

And now, he was sitting poolside at the island resort

hotel where Cher would soon marry the blue collar man of her dreams, much to their parents' dismay. Elliot wanted to stand up and cheer every time he thought about it. He'd always admired Cher's independent streak. He'd just never had much desire to emulate it. Until recently.

His life bored him, plain and simple. It was shallow. Empty. Filled with friends who weren't really his friends and women who only wanted him for what he could buy them. His "job" running the family charity was mostly something his parents let him do so he'd have something on his resume. And so far, he'd hardly done anything with it. To be honest, he'd barely done enough with the charity to qualify as work. But for months now, he'd been trying to rectify that situation. His parents, however, were used to how things were run and weren't too enthused about changing things.

He could charm the cash out of the cold-hearted clutches of their friends at the annual fundraiser without breaking a sweat, and they were more than happy for him to keep doing that. But it wasn't enough for him anymore. The money was ferried out to so many different charities he doubted it really made a difference to any of them. And it should. He wanted to up the game. But they'd shot down every idea he'd come up with for redirecting or expanding the charity, dismissing him without even listening.

He took a sip of ice water and frowned. Refreshing, but not nearly strong enough to dull the raw mass of depression that had been eating at his gut since he and his parents had had their last little talk. It had surprised the hell out of him that he actually cared about running the charity. Sure, it had always been a great way to get chicks. Everyone loved a philanthropist, right? But ever since the last charity event, where he'd actually met some of the kids that they donated to, there had been a niggling feeling in the back of his mind that he wanted to do more. He suddenly wanted to make a difference. Perhaps it would make his parents happy if he promised them he'd raise double the money they brought in last year. He needed to prove to them that he was more than just a spoiled playboy, or he'd be stuck in this rut forever and an even worse waste of space than he currently was.

"God, you're a morbid son of a bitch," he muttered to himself, taking another swig of water.

"Hey, there, mind if I sit down?" The brunette from earlier sat down on the chaise next to him, apparently having worked up the nerve to approach.

Elliot plastered his charmer smile on his face, shoving down all the unpleasant emotions roiling through his system. He couldn't run from it forever, but for a few minutes at least, flirting with a beautiful woman might make him forget about his parents, his so-called job, and his boring life.

"Not at all." He sat up and held out his hand. "I'm Elliot Debusshere."

"Stacy Connors," she said, slowly sliding her hand into his so her fingertips lingered along every inch of his hand and palm before coming to a rest.

Nice move. He wondered how long she'd practiced it and then gave himself a mental kick. He didn't even know her. She might be a perfectly genuine person.

"Would you like a drink?" he asked, waving a waiter over.

"That would be great, thanks. It's hot out today." She flipped her thick, chocolate-hued hair over her shoulder, giving him a better view of her body beneath her skimpy lace cover-up.

He didn't miss the quick glance she raked over him, taking in not only the body he made sure looked impressive, but also the expensive watch on his wrist, his designer sunglasses, and the number to the penthouse suite he told the waiter to bill her drink to.

He knew her type. And usually he'd be very interested. But for some reason, he couldn't keep his mind on her or the nonsense coming out of her mouth.

Elliot's gaze wandered over the other guests enjoying the deluxe pool grounds. Water slides flowed from fake mountains, and an aquarium was set into one side of the pool, which gave the guests the illusion of literally swimming with the fishes—and a few sharks, if he wasn't mistaken. There were a lot more kids around than he was used to.

The hotel had other pools he could have chosen. But this one, with its waterfall and palm trees sprinkled liberally around, had felt more tropical, like he was relaxing in some jungle oasis rather than at a five star resort.

The woman beside him asked him something, and he turned to ask her to repeat the question when he caught sight of a total knockout standing ankle deep in the opposite side of the pool. But what had caught his attention wasn't the fact that her modest, one-piece swimsuit clung to her like plum-colored perfection, accenting her blond coloring and showcasing her beauty in a way that the skimpiest bikini never could have. Or even the fanny pack she wore around her waist— Who wore those anymore? It was the look of sheer terror on her face.

Her eyes were wide, staring at a little boy standing in the shallow water near the aquarium.

"Tyler!" she shouted. "Get out of the pool right now!"

Stacy *tsked*. "Some people. If you can't control your kids, you shouldn't bring them out in public."

Any interest Elliot might have had in her evaporated.

"I'm sorry, but I've got to go. If you'll excuse me," he said. He stood and gave her a sharp nod before heading toward the pool.

The woman had waded a little farther in. Her face was completely bloodless, so pale even her lips had lost their color. Her gaze darted from the child to the surrounding water like they were standing in a river of molten lava instead of a pool not more than three feet deep.

Elliot wasn't sure what he could do to help, but he was going to find out.

Lena paced back and forth near the edge of the hotel pool, her heart pounding in her throat. The pool sported a large ramp that sloped gently into deeper water instead of the typical cement lip and the water lapped gently at her toes. That was as far as she'd go. Under normal circumstances. She and any body of water, no matter how large or small, did not mix. Ever. And if Tyler wouldn't get out, she wasn't sure what she was going to do.

"Tyler Nathaniel, you get out of the pool right now!" she called again.

Tyler, nearly drunk with joy over his first foray into a massive, watery wonderland, pretended not to hear her.

She couldn't really blame him. The pool had been designed as a child's fantasyland come to life. Waterfalls, water spouts, and jets sprouted out in every direction. One wall of the pool even butted up to an aquarium. The wall was thick Plexiglass, enabling the kids to "swim" with the exotic fish.

While Lena knew there was no logical chance of the fish and her child actually touching one another, she'd done her best to steer Tyler clear of that wall. No need to make the whole swimming thing even more dangerous than it already was. Especially for an inexperienced kid like Tyler. Heck, he'd never done more than run through the sprinklers in their backyard before. Even those little plastic baby pools had been too much for her to handle.

But when he'd seen the amazing pool at the hotel where they were staying for her brother Oz's wedding, Tyler had begged her and she'd finally given in. After all, swimming was a totally normal part of life. For most people. And she didn't want to inflict all her fears on her child. But still... What if she couldn't get him out?

Panic clawed at her throat, and she choked back tears. He was having a good time and theoretically, she knew he was safe. With a life vest and arm floaties, he wasn't likely to drown in the waist-deep water he stood in. Especially with a lifeguard on duty. But it was time to go, he wasn't interested in leaving, and she couldn't go in to get him.

"Tyler!" she called again, trying to keep the fear from her voice. She didn't want to freak anyone out. He ducked under another waterfall, his laughter echoing from behind the water.

"Come on, Tyler, we need to go. You can come back later."

"Ten more minutes!"

"No, Tyler, now!"

He giggled and ran farther off, water spraying around him as he splashed away.

She hated resorting to bribes and usually didn't need to. Tyler was a pretty good kid. But enough was enough. At that moment, she'd promise him anything as long as he got out of the damn pool.

"Tyler, it's time to go get some ice cream! Don't you want to go get a nice, big hot fudge sundae? You can get extra sprinkles."

"No, I wanna swim!" he said, splashing around.

That surprised her. Tyler loved ice cream more than any other food in the world. Okay. Bigger ammo.

"I'll let you stay up past your bedtime tonight."

No response at all.

"You can play the Xbox that's in our room!"

That one made him pause. She didn't usually allow him to play video games. Finding an Xbox in their hotel room had been the highlight of the trip for him until he realized he wouldn't get to play it here, either. She was sure that bribe would work. And it looked like it might until one of the other kids excitedly shrieked. A shark had come up to the glass for a visit, and all the kids were getting as close as they dared. A huge grin broke out on Tyler's face, and he headed straight for the wall.

Terror flooded through Lena. The water was now up to Tyler's waist. And there was a freaking shark ten feet away from him! She didn't care if there was glass between them. She wanted her baby out of that pool, now!

"Tyler!" She knew her panic was showing. She was drawing stares from other parents. One of the lifeguards had taken notice and was assessing the situation, unsure what to do, since no one was actually in danger. Well, maybe she was, from hyperventilating. She couldn't seem to draw a deep breath.

"Tyler, get out right now! I'll take you shopping. You can pick out any toy you want."

Nothing. He didn't even look at her.

"How about we get you your very own Xbox? Do you want to go get an Xbox? You can play it every day!"

His little hand pressed against the glass, and Lena's heart jumped into her throat. Her stomach roiled. She slid a foot farther into the water, her whole body trembling. It was up to her ankle. She hadn't had any part of her body completely submerged since she was two years old and had almost drowned in her grandparents' hot tub. She'd taken off her arm floaties when her mom wasn't watching and had stepped right in. And had immediately sunk. She didn't even remember the exact incident. But every time she got near any body of water, she could feel the pressure of all that liquid weight crushing her, pushing her down to the bottom, just like it had that day. Why did she let her own child traipse right into a watery death trap from which she couldn't extract him? What kind of mother was she? And how the hell was she going to get her son when she could barely force herself to put more than her foot in the water?

There were enough people in the pool... Maybe she could convince a few to line up so she could walk across their heads. Or have them pass her around like in some concert mosh pit. She'd even ask a nice, strong guy to give her a piggy back ride if it would get her to Tyler without having to go in the water any deeper.

The boy laughed and pounded on the glass. The shark

jerked and swished its tail.

"Tyler! Get out right now," she shouted, no longer caring who was watching.

The lifeguard climbed a few steps down from his tower, still confused but obviously wanting to get her and her kid away from the pool before she had a full-on panic attack. He'd better hurry.

Before he could get all the way off his tower, a leanly muscled man with artfully tousled hair and a smile on his face that would charm a used car salesman, came up to him. He clapped the lifeguard on the back and said something to him that made the guard nod and climb back up his tower.

No, no, no! He needs to rescue Tyler! Lena slid her other foot into the pool, closing her eyes briefly against the wave of terror that strangled her. She waded in up to her shins, biting her lip to keep back the whimpering scream that crawled up her throat. Black spots flickered at her vision, and the world tilted slightly, but she fought it back, sucking in one breath after another until the world righted itself. She needed to get to her son.

The man who'd spoken to the lifeguard yanked his shirt over his head and kicked off his flip-flops. He waded into the pool, aimed a megawatt smile at her, and held up a hand in a slight wave. Her stomach unclenched a fraction. He looked a bit familiar. Actually, he reminded her of Cher, her soon-to-be sister-in-law. They had the same hair color, similar features. But she hadn't met him before. Still, something about him calmed her a bit. He waded across the pool toward Tyler, and Lena almost collapsed, her head swimming with unreleased adrenaline and overwhelming relief.

She backed out of the water, her body relaxing a few

more degrees now that it was no longer imminently in danger from drowning. And yes, she knew that was an exaggeration, but at that moment she didn't care.

The man made it to Tyler. He leaned down to talk to him. Tyler immediately grabbed his hand and dragged him closer to the glass. Lena closed her eyes and groaned. She'd given Tyler the stranger-danger talk a million times and still he was *way* too friendly with strangers. Especially men. And no, he probably wasn't in any danger from the kind, charismatic man who was crouched in the water pointing at fish with him, but still. You never knew. He should have at least looked back to her for permission to speak to him.

They talked a little more, and then Tyler jumped up and down, a huge grin on his face. He held his arms up to the man who swung Tyler up on his shoulders and started walking toward her. Tyler looked so natural sitting up on the man's shoulders, giggling and chatting away. She'd have to take the man out to dinner or something to thank him for rescuing her baby.

The world spun around her again, and she wasn't sure if it was from sheer and utter relief that Tyler was safely out of the water, the insanely hot sun she'd been standing in for the better part of the afternoon, the fact that she'd been up to her shins in water for the first time in twenty-four years, or the realization that the tempting man with the amazing smile had an incredible body to match. Her panic had eclipsed anything else, including the toned muscles and broad shoulders of her new hero. But with her son safely out of harm's way, it was hard *not* to notice. The man had the body of a freaking god, all tanned and hard, streams of water running down his chest and glistening in the sun.

The stranger took Tyler down from his shoulders, and his smile warmed the residual ice from her blood that Tyler's stunt and her own little foray into the pool had put there. Her son's hand slipped into hers. She looked up at the man to say thank you.

The last thing she saw was the smile dropping off his face before everything went black.

Chapter Two

Elliot carried the woozy woman into his room, her little boy following anxiously behind.

"Is Mommy going to be okay?"

Elliot glanced down, feeling like he had in grade school whenever the teacher had called on him to answer a question he couldn't answer—squirming with anxiety and no clue what to say. He sure as hell hoped the woman was okay because he had no idea what to do with the kid.

"No worries, little man. She'll be fine. I promise."

He laid her down on the bed, making sure her head was cradled comfortably on the pillows. She looked up at him, squinting like she couldn't quite make him out. Then she sighed and closed her eyes. Within seconds, a faint snore emanated from her perfect heart-shaped mouth. His eyebrows rose, and he glanced back at the boy who giggled.

"Mommy's snoring."

Elliot bit back a laugh, held his finger up to his lips, and mock whispered, "Let's be quiet so she can sleep."

The boy nodded and clapped his lips together. He stood staring at Elliot. At a total loss, Elliot turned back to the woman. He took off her fanny pack—the fact that she wore one had probably shocked him more than her fainting into his arms—pulled a light blanket up over her and stood back. Her blond curls spread over the pillows like a halo. Her full lips were slightly parted, and he had the sudden urge to lean down and kiss her.

He almost snorted. The last chick he'd dated had been disturbingly into fairy tales and had made him watch a lot of Disney films. Casting himself in the roll of Prince Charming wasn't something that had ever entered his mind before.

The little boy climbed up next to his mother and patted her cheek.

"Mommy," he whispered.

When she didn't respond, he looked up at Elliot, his blue eyes open wide.

The lifeguard had checked her out and had figured it was probably heat exhaustion combined with a possible panic attack, if the look on her face when she'd waded into the pool had been any indication. He'd recommended taking her to her room and calling the hotel doc. Elliot wasn't real sure about hauling a nauseous, hysterical woman with a kid into his hotel room, but he'd done what the lifeguard suggested. The front desk assured him the doctor was on the way. Hopefully, the man would get there soon.

"What's your mom's name?" he asked the boy.

"Mommy."

Elliot grinned. "I know, but what's her real name? What do other people call her?"

His nose wrinkled. "Uncle Oz calls her Lenny, but Mommy doesn't like that."

Elliot laughed. "Lenny, huh. Oh. Uncle Oz? Is your uncle Nathaniel Oserkowski?"

"Yup. That's my name, too. Tyler Nathaniel Oserkowski."

"Good to meet you, little dude. I'm Elliot Debusshere."

"My name's not dude. It's Tyler."

"Oh. Okay. Sorry. Hi, Tyler."

Tyler just looked at him. *Okay then.* Elliot cleared his throat. "I'm your aunt Cherice's brother."

That got a grin out of him. "Aunt Cher!"

"Yep. So it looks like we're family."

Tyler's face scrunched in confusion at that new concept.

There was a knock on the door, and Elliot hurried over to let the doctor in.

After a quick exam and diagnosis of mild heat exhaustion and anxiety, the doctor left with orders for rest and water, and he was once again alone with Tyler. Once the boy had been assured his mother would be okay, he'd turned his attention to his surroundings. Elliot watched the little kid wander around, poking into corners, looking into cabinets.

He pulled out his phone and dialed his sister, his fingers drumming on his leg until she picked up.

"Hey Elliot, how's it going?" Cher said.

He exhaled, relieved she'd answered. "Not great. I ran into Oz's sister at the pool. She had a bit of a panic attack and then passed out from heat exhaustion."

"Oh my gosh, is she okay?"

"Yeah, the doc said she'd be fine. She woke up long enough to get some fluids in her, but she's resting in my room right now."

"Good thing you were there! Is Tyler with you?"

"Yeah." Elliot turned his back and walked to the other side of the room so Tyler couldn't hear him. "Can you guys come get him?"

"Sorry, bro. Oz and I are meeting with the minister in ten minutes."

Elliot's stomach twisted. "But... I don't know anything about kids. What am I going to do with him?"

Cher laughed. "He's just a kid, Elliot, not a rabid wolf. Give him a snack and put a movie on for him or something. He'll be fine."

"Yeah, but..."

"He's a little...on the precocious side. Really smart. Just talk to him. If you get him going on something he likes, he can talk forever."

"Great."

"Oh, stop." Cher sighed. "Talk about cars. He likes cars."

"Cars, huh? Okay. But what—"

"Oh, the minister is here. I've got to run. If the doctor isn't worried, I'm sure Lena will be up soon. Play with him. He's a good kid. Talk to you later!"

The phone clicked off before Elliot could argue more. "Shit," he muttered.

He turned around to find Tyler sitting on the floor in front of the mini-fridge, surrounded by all the contents.

"Tyler! What are you doing?" He'd taken his eyes off him for one minute. How did he get into so much so fast?

"You said a bad word," Tyler said, clutching a mini-bottle of champagne in each hand.

"Ah! Give me those." Elliot lunged for him, but Tyler dropped the bottles and moved on to a mini-bottle of vodka.

Shit. Lena was going to kill him. He'd been alone with Tyler for sixty seconds, and the kid was juggling booze.

"I'm hungry," Tyler said.

What the hell do kids eat? He glanced at the pile of food on the floor. "Here," Elliot said, tossing him a bag of chips.

Tyler tore into them with a look of pure ecstasy on his face. Elliot took advantage of the reprieve to gather up the remaining anti-kid snacks and drinks to hide them in a high cupboard. When he turned back around, only the back half of Tyler was visible. The other half was buried in the entertainment center.

"Whoa, little dude, what are you doing?"

"Can we play?" he asked, pulling out an Xbox controller.

Relief flooded through Elliot. Finally, something he knew how to do.

"Sure!"

Tyler's face lit up like Elliot was his new best friend. "Yay!"

"What do you want to play?"

Elliott pulled out a stack of games, shuffling through them and discarding them just as quickly. He always made sure he had a hotel room that came fully stocked with some entertainment, but he'd never had to worry about having kid-friendly stuff before. The only game he had that wasn't rated *M* was Minecraft. And that was probably a bit advanced for Tyler.

"How old are you, kid?"

"Six and a half."

Elliot raised an eyebrow. He would have guessed younger. Then again, he'd never been close enough to an almost seven-year-old, so what did he know?

"You want to play this one?"

"Sure! All my friends play that one." Tyler bounced up and down on the couch.

"Okay, okay. Settle down. Here, go grab yourself some of those snacks while I get everything hooked up."

"Yippee!" Tyler scurried down and snatched up an armload of chips, cookies, and soda and plopped back down on the couch.

He'd consumed half of it by the time Elliot had everything ready to go. Wow. And Elliot thought *he* could eat. This kid could chow him under the table.

"That good?" he asked as Tyler shoved a barbeque chip he'd dipped in a jar of Nutella into his mouth.

"Super yummy. Wanna try?" he asked, holding out another interesting specimen.

"Um, no thanks. Do you even know what that stuff is?"

Tyler shrugged and jammed it into his mouth. "No, but Mommy says it has good protein and vitmins."

"Vitamins?"

"Yep."

"I didn't know that."

"I know lots of stuff."

"You do?"

Tyler nodded, sending his blond curls flopping all over and a shower of crumbs onto the couch. "Yup. Especially about sharks. I know lots about them."

"Yeah? Sharks are pretty cool."

"Yeah! Have you seen *Jaws*?"

Elliot raised an eyebrow. "Yes. Have you?"

"Yeah. But don't tell my mommy. I'm not 'posed to watch stuff like that. I saw it when Uncle Oz fell asleep watching me."

"Ah. Okay. I won't say a word."

"Do you have music?"

Wow. The kid was barely taking a breath. "Yeah," Elliot said. "I've got some in here. You want to listen?"

"You got Johnny Cash?"

That one had Elliot's eyes widening again. "You like Johnny Cash?"

"Oh yeah, he's the best. But Mommy says I can't play him for a while 'cause she gots a headache. So maybe we shouldn't listen to him right now, since she doesn't feel good."

"That might be a good idea."

"She likes the face song, though."

"The face song?"

"The one where he sings about seeing her face. Mommy likes that one. But she says when you hear it, you have ta dance with a girl. I dance with her in the kitchen sometimes."

It had been just five minutes and exhaustion already pulled at Elliot. Where the hell did all the energy come from? Another hour and he'd probably be down with a migraine from the sheer volume of words coming out of the kid's mouth, but Tyler was kind of a crack-up. And Elliot could envision the beautiful woman currently lying in his bed dancing around the kitchen with her son. It was an appealing picture.

"You do? Well that's very nice of you," Elliot said.

"Yeah. Mommy says I should be a gentleman."

"Well, she's right. A gentleman is a good thing to be."

"Yeah." He put his head to the side, his little nose scrunched up. "But I don't wanna dance with other girls. Just Mommy."

Elliot laughed. "It can be fun dancing with girls."

Tyler grimaced like someone was trying to force feed him lima beans. "Do you dance with girls?"

"Every chance I get," he said, wiggling his eyebrows.

Tyler made a gagging face. "Girls are gross."

Elliot thought about the woman sleeping in his bed. "You won't always think so."

"I just dance with Mommy, if she wants."

"Well, I'm sure your mommy loves dancing with you."

"Yeah. Hey, do you have a car? Does it go fast?"

Elliot opened his mouth to answer, but Tyler kept talking. "I'm going to get a real fast car when I'm bigger. There's a couple of us at home that are going to race when we get cars. Only, one kid backed out of the race so far. He fell off his bike when we raced those, so his mom won't let him race anymore."

Elliot's ribs were beginning to hurt from the laughter threatening to erupt. If he let it out, he was never going to stop, and he didn't want to hurt the kid's feelings or anything. "You're going to race, huh?"

"Yeah, I set that up already. Don't tell Mommy that, either."

Elliot nodded with exaggerated solemnity. "Deal. Hey," he said quickly, before Tyler could start off on another tangent, "why don't we play the game?"

"Oooh, yeah, I wanna play!"

Elliot handed him the controller. "Okay, little man. Let's get our game on."

L ena woke in a strange bed, buried deep in pillows with a cool breeze from the air conditioner blowing over her. She sat up slowly, a horrific headache pounding away at her skull.

Tyler!

All her aches and pains were eclipsed by a rush of panic. She swung her feet out of the bed, pausing when she heard Tyler's laughter ringing through the room. She jumped up and hurried through the open double doors into a spacious living room. The hotel suite was decked out like a luxury apartment. In fact, it was bigger than the apartment where she'd lived before she and Tyler had moved in with her brother.

Tyler laughed again, and she looked over the couch to see him playing video games on a huge widescreen TV with a gorgeous man. Correction—the gorgeous god from the pool. Who apparently passed the time playing video games. Okay.

"Yeah! High five me, buddy," the man said.

He held his hand up for Tyler to slap and then looked over his shoulder and saw her standing there. He passed the game controller over to Tyler. "Take over for me, buddy, okay? I'll be right back. I wanna talk to your mom."

Tyler looked over his shoulder. "I'm going to build a new room in the castle, kay? Hey, Mom!" He grinned at her, showing a mouthful of Oreo-encrusted teeth.

She sucked back a groan. "You okay?"

"Yep!"

The man hurried over to her.

"The kid's a total natural. He's already beat some creepers and built a whole new wing onto my castle. It took me a month to figure out how to do half the stuff he's doing. I'll never hear the end of it if my friends find out."

Lena's eyes widened a little in surprise. "Your friends know you play video games?"

His smile faded around the edges, and Lena flushed. "I'm sorry. I only meant... Well, I usually don't let him play video games."

And the fact that this guy had not only let him play video games but had spent the afternoon pumping him full of sugar and junk food and playing with him meant that Tyler would probably be completely obsessed with him. Tyler had a tendency to latch on to men, any man, who paid attention to him. Oz was a great father figure for him, but it wasn't quite the same as having a real dad, and Oz was always so busy, even he didn't always get to spend a lot of time with Tyler. The last thing Lena wanted was for Tyler to get attached to some random guy. The fact that he was beyond hot, and Lena wanted to get attached to him herself, was even worse.

The guy jammed his hand through his hair, the wary expression on his face reminded her of Tyler when he was caught doing something naughty.

"I'm sorry," he said. "He didn't say he wasn't allowed, and I didn't think to ask. He saw the console when we brought you up and wanted to play. I didn't have much else here to entertain him, and he was getting into everything."

She snorted. "Yeah, he's good at that."

Lena rose up onto her toes to see better over the couch, frowning at the pile of junk food surrounding Tyler. His little hand dove into a bowl of chips, and he promptly shoved them into his mouth.

"Tyler, no more junk food, baby. It's probably almost

time for dinner."

Tyler groaned, but he kept his hand out of the chips.

"Sorry," the man said again. "He was hungry, so I let him pick out some snacks. Since you were asleep, I didn't want to wake you to ask what he usually ate."

Lena swallowed back the lecture on proper child nutrition. The guy obviously wasn't used to being around children. She should be thankful that her son was still in the hotel room in one piece.

"No. That's okay. Really. I mean, I don't usually let him eat junk food. He gets a little crazy when sugar gets into his system, so I usually stick to fruits, and cheese, and…" Lena stopped at the man's growing concern. "Don't worry about it. It was kind of you to take care of him."

The sudden smolder in his eyes warmed her down to her toes. "My pleasure. He's a great kid. We had fun."

Yeah, that was what worried her. It was going to be embarrassing if she had to pry her kid off some stranger's leg.

He looked her over, his eyes narrowing in concern. "How are you feeling?"

"A little headache, but better. Thanks."

"Glad to hear it. You gave me a scare there for a second," he said, leaning in to give her arm a gentle squeeze with a half smile that set a few thousand butterflies loose in her stomach. "I'm Elliot, by the way. Debusshere. Cherice's brother."

Relief flooded through Lena that her child hadn't been in the care of some stranger all afternoon. Well, he was a stranger, technically, but he was almost family so… That was better. Kind of. No, actually, it was worse. That meant they'd be seeing him all week. A week of the kind of attention Tyler had just gotten, and her poor little boy would be crushed when it was time to go home and he realized Elliot wasn't his to keep. She needed to make sure Tyler knew it had been a one-time deal.

"I'm Lena, Oz's sister," she said, sticking her hand out.

He squeezed her hand as he shook it. His hand was warm and smooth and at least twice the size of hers. And he held it quite a bit longer than politeness demanded. "Yes, the bridesmaid. I'm the groomsman, at your service," he said with a little bow.

The butterflies kicked into high gear. She clenched her ab muscles trying to squash the damn things. They had no business showing up to throw a kink into her life.

"Nice to meet you. Officially," she said in what she hoped was a pleasant but casual tone.

"My pleasure," he said again. "Tyler mentioned his Uncle Oz a few times, so I figured that's who you were. I called my sister to make sure Oz knew where you two were."

"Oh, good. Thank you."

"No problem. I was hoping we'd meet up before all the wedding festivities got into full swing. Didn't want our first meeting to be when I escorted you down the aisle," he said, waggling his eyebrows.

The sudden image of them walking down the aisle with her dressed in a gorgeous white gown instead of the mint-green bridesmaid number she'd wear that weekend had Lena's cheeks flaming again. Where the hell did that come from? She'd known the guy, what, five minutes? Usually, the married-happily-ever-after fantasies took a few weeks to start running rampant. Though, really, he'd kept Tyler entertained, and he was funny and drop dead gorgeous. She'd certainly done a lot worse.

Then again, Elliot really wasn't relationship material. Lena had heard stories from Cher. Stories that were funny when told over family dinners, but not so funny when her child was in danger of becoming too attached. Elliot was much more the sweep-them-off-their-feet-love-'em-then-leave-'em type. Different girl on his arm every week. Not the type a single mother needed to be messing with.

Thankfully, Elliot had turned his attention back to Tyler and didn't seem to notice her momentary flusterfication.

"Tyler's been telling me all about being the ring bearer," he said.

Tyler didn't take his eyes off the game but called over his shoulder. "I have ta carry them on a pillow, and I have ta go slow so I don't drop 'em. Elliot showed me."

Elliot laughed. "You're going to do great." He turned back to Lena. "We practiced a little."

"Yep!" chimed in Tyler.

Lena's heart was in danger of melting around the edges. Until she reminded herself that no matter how hot or charming the man in front of her was, he was a headache, or heartache, waiting to happen. For her and Tyler. She shoved her hair behind her ear and looked around the room. Anywhere but directly at the handsome hunk-of-a-hero in front of her. She needed to steer clear. "So, what happened? I passed out?"

"Yeah. Damn near gave me a heart attack. I almost didn't catch you."

"Sorry about that," she mumbled.

Her cheeks burned, both in mortification that she'd

dropped like a fly for no real reason and at the thought that he'd caught her. And carried her up to his hotel room where he had tucked her into his bed. Where he slept, probably naked as gorgeous hunks do. In her fantasies, at least.

She swallowed and tried desperately to get a grip. She was drooling over the poor guy like she'd never seen one before. Her gaze raked over him while she pondered that thought for a second. To be fair, she *hadn't* seen one quite so well put together before. At least not close up. Still. She needed to chill the hell out.

He laughed, an easy going, happy sound that eased her embarrassment. There was something about him that was extremely comforting. Well, aside from the high school crush-like tingles running riot through her body. But instead of wanting to die from sheer humiliation because she'd passed out while her son had been in two feet of water, Elliot made it seem like a normal, everyday occurrence that was no big deal. He was very sweet.

Too sweet. Tyler was already looking at the guy with a mild case of hero worship that was only going to get worse.

"It was no problem at all, really. I had the hotel doctor come up. He said you probably have a mild case of heat exhaustion. He gave you some fluids and a little something to help sleep it off. You should be feeling much better in a few hours, but he suggested taking it easy and said to make sure you drink lots of water. Oh, speaking of which…"

Elliot hurried to the small fridge and pulled out a bottle of water. "Here you go. Drink up. Doctor's orders."

His light brown eyes had such a lighthearted twinkle in them Lena couldn't help but give him a grudging smile.

"Yes, sir," she said, cracking the lid off the bottle and

taking a sip.

"Tyler was telling me you don't really like the water. Pools and things, I mean."

Lena's cheeks grew warm. "Yeah, that's a bit of an understatement."

"*Hmm*. And you're about to spend an entire week at a beachside resort, surrounded by them."

Lena's mouth went dry. "Yeah," she managed to squeak out. She cleared her throat and tried again. "My best friend was supposed to be here to help with Tyler. Take him to the pool and the beach and basically wrangle him while I'm busy with wedding stuff."

She repressed a shudder, barely. "But when I called her this morning, her flight had been delayed due to weather, so I'm not sure when, or if, she'll make it. And Tyler wanted to swim so badly. There's a view of the pools from our room, and it looked so fun. And I don't want him growing up with the same issues I have, so I thought it would be okay if I took him down for a few minutes. But then he wouldn't get out…"

Elliot took her hand and gave it a reassuring squeeze. "No worries. I'm glad I was there to help."

Lena tore her gaze from Elliot and focused on Tyler. Who was still playing video games and had been for who knew how long. It was past time for them to leave.

"Well, Elliot, thanks again. Really. We'd… We'd better be going. Tyler, clean up your mess, please."

"Ahhh," he grumbled.

"It's not tragic, make it magic," she said, using the little prompt she'd made up for him to get him to clean up. "Mary Poppins it."

"Okay!" Tyler popped up and started snapping his fingers and running around like a loon while he picked things up and ran to put them away.

Elliot's mouth dropped open a little, and Lena laughed.

"It looks crazy but it works," she said. "I can't make stuff magically clean itself up like Mary Poppins does, but he snaps and pretends it's happening magically."

They watched as Tyler snapped over an empty bag of chips and then scooped it up and shoved it into the trash as fast as he could. He was done cleaning up his mess in two minutes flat.

Elliot leaned against the couch with his arms crossed over his chest, watching the action. He turned to her and nodded. "Impressive."

"Thanks." Lena held out her hand to her son. "Tyler, let's go, bud."

"Okay, Mommy," he said, sighing the sigh of a child being made to do something he didn't want to do but knowing it was no use arguing. Good thing, too. He'd already gotten away with a lion's share of mischief.

"Can I come play again?"

"Sur—" Elliot stopped and looked at Lena, eyebrows raised in question.

"We'll see," she said again, with a slight frown.

Tyler sighed. "That means no."

"No. It means we'll see."

Though he was right. It meant no. At least in this case. She'd always hated it when her mother had used that phrase. But it was handy when she didn't want to say no outright. It got her off the hook long enough that she didn't have to be the bad guy. At the moment, at least.

"Well, I guess I'll see you soon," Elliot said, walking them to the door. "I think Oz and Cherice have a family dinner planned."

"Yeah. We'll see you there."

"Looking forward to it," he said, his eyes locking on to hers.

Lena's heart clenched again. She'd never be able to resist a whole week of that. Was it bad form to hook up with the groomsman at your brother's wedding? She'd have to Google some wedding etiquette.

Chapter Three

Elliot closed the door behind Lena and Tyler, his head completely in an uproar. What the hell had just happened? Crazy coincidence that hot-as-hell Panic Attack Lady had ended up being Oz's sister. He'd never have guessed they were siblings, though he supposed they looked enough alike. Aside from the height thing. Oz was an inch or two taller than Elliot, at six-foot-one. Lena definitely got the short end of the stick in the height department. She probably wasn't more than five-foot-six at the most, with curly, blond hair and sparkling blue eyes that lit up every time she looked at her son. Not his usual type, by a long stretch. He liked his women exotic, mysterious, and uninterested in anything more than a fling. No single mothers. Ever.

Not that he didn't like kids. He did. He just had no direct experience with them. Like at all.

But to his surprise, he'd enjoyed hanging out with Tyler while they'd waited for Lena to wake up. The kid was a riot.

And a hell of a lot smarter than he'd assumed an almost seven-year-old would be. He wouldn't mind hanging with him again. And he really wouldn't mind seeing Lena again. A thought that should scare the hell out of him. She was a single mom. Mad respect to her. But Elliot could barely run his own life. The last thing he wanted to do was mess with anyone with a kid. Lena should be firmly on his off-limits list.

But he couldn't stop thinking about the look on her face in the pool. The only thing he'd wanted to do was help her, protect her. And the feel of her in his arms when he'd laid her in his bed...small and soft and utterly his, for that moment at least. That was something he'd like to feel again.

But he had zero business getting involved with someone like her. Elliot was no good for either of them, and he knew it. But the fact that their siblings were getting married, and they were stuck together on an island with all the pre-wedding festivities, was going to make avoiding her damn near impossible. Especially since he couldn't pretend, even to himself, that he really wanted to avoid her.

By the time dinner rolled around, he'd definitely decided that pursuing Lena would not be in either of their best interests. However, five seconds after Lena walked in, he regretted that decision. Big time. She looked incredible in a blue, sleeveless sundress that almost exactly matched the shade of her eyes. Her hair was pulled into a haphazard bun that left little tendrils escaping down her neck. His fingers itched to wrap those locks around his fingers, see if they were really as silky as they looked.

Well, he didn't have to pursue her, but it probably wouldn't hurt to be friendly. They were going to be family, sort of, after all.

It only took about two minutes of the meal for him to realize Lena had avoidance plans of her own. She entered the room, and although there were two seats right next to him, she headed to the opposite side of the table. Tyler, however, spotted him and refused to move once he planted himself next to Elliot, so Lena reluctantly followed.

Elliot had his reasons for avoiding her, but the thought that she wanted to keep her distance made the perverse anti-authority side of him want to redouble his efforts at getting her attention. Reverse psychology at its best. Of course, the fact that he wanted her to want him confused the hell out of him. Her disinterest should have been a good thing. So why did his gut twist in a knot every time she looked away or avoided his attempts at conversation?

The resort had a live band playing tropical versions of non-tropical songs that Elliot had done his best to tune out. They weren't bad. Just not his thing. But when they segued into a Johnny Cash song, Tyler shot to his feet.

"Mommy! It's the face song. You gotta dance!"

Lena's pale cheeks flushed red, but she didn't argue. She stood and took her son's hand. He climbed onto her feet, put one hand on her waist and held the other, and they danced as a man with a thick island accent crooned about the first time he ever saw her face.

Cher leaned over to Elliot. "Oz told me she's been singing this song to Tyler since the day he was born. They are so adorable."

Elliot turned his attention back to Lena and her son. Yes, they were adorable. And it was obvious how close they were. Even more reason for him to leave them the hell alone. But he couldn't. Even though if things went south with her, it wouldn't just be her life he messed up.

The song ended, and Tyler bounced back to the table.

"You are an excellent dancer, little man," Elliot said, high-fiving him.

"Thanks." Tyler shoved a piece of pineapple into his mouth. "Do you want to dance with my mommy?"

Elliot opened his mouth to say no but couldn't seem to get the words out. The truth was he'd love to dance with her. He just couldn't. Or shouldn't. But oh yes, he wanted to.

Not that it mattered. Lena beat him to it. "No, Tyler. We don't need to bother Elliot. Besides, I'm all danced out." She smiled down at her son, and the sheer beauty of her in that moment had a small headache forming between Elliot's eyes.

The internal fight between wanting to charm his way into Lena's life and knowing he should do no such thing was going to make his head implode.

Perhaps he was going about it all wrong. They didn't need to have a relationship. He was no good for her and wouldn't have the first clue what to do with a child in his life. But he'd caught her eye on him when she thought he wasn't looking, so she wasn't totally immune to him. And while they were on the island, their real lives were put on hold. Why couldn't they have a little fun together?

"So, have you ever been to the island before?" he asked her, determined to capture her attention.

Lena yanked a sugar packet from Tyler's mouth and

barely spared a glance for Elliot. "No, I don't travel much."

"That's too bad. Well, you'll have to make the most of it while you're here then."

"Huh?" she said, squinting at him. "Tyler, put that down and sit in your seat," she said, grabbing a coconut that Tyler had snagged from the centerpiece in front of them.

"I said you'll have to make the most of it while you're here," he repeated.

"Oh. Yeah." She yanked Tyler back into his seat with one hand and rescued a nearly overturned cup of water with the other. Multi-tasking at its best.

"So, if you don't travel much, what do you do for fun?" he asked, trying another line of questioning.

She gave a short, humorless laugh and snagged the knife Tyler was trying to cut the table with and placed it out of reach. "I don't really have much time for fun."

She kept her attention on her son and his antics, avoiding eye contact and interaction with him whenever possible. She answered any questions he asked her, but despite turning on the charm higher than he'd ever had to before, he couldn't pull her into a conversation. Granted, she continued to have her hands full with Tyler. The kid was a hyper ball of energy. He bounced in his seat, climbed under the table a few times, and almost over it once.

Since the sugar rush that had apparently hijacked the little boy's system was 100 percent his fault, Elliot tried to assuage his guilt by helping to distract him. But his efforts only succeeded in Tyler climbing all over him until Oz finally got up, plucked Tyler from Elliot's shoulders where he'd lodged himself, and plunked him into his seat. A stern warning, complete with finger waving and the parental look-of-death, and Tyler settled into his seat to pout. Wow. Impressive.

Tyler perked up once the food came. A boy after his own heart. While the kid was busy stuffing his face with pulled pork, Elliot tried again to draw Lena into some kind of conversation. But she barely paid attention to him. She fussed with her plate, with Tyler's plate, and with Tyler himself until the kid finally groaned in exasperation and she let him alone. She did nothing overtly rude or standoffish, but she more than got the point across that she wasn't interested.

He'd never, in his twenty-six years of life, *ever* had a woman ignore him so completely. Usually, one glance and she was his. But since flirting, winking, casual, innocent brushes of his body against hers, and all the other tricks in his bag weren't working, perhaps he should try being direct and asking her out?

He hesitated, a weird sensation in the pit of his stomach. It took him a moment, but he finally realized he was nervous. That realization surprised him enough that he sat there for a second, unsure of how to proceed. The thought that she might actually turn him down was so foreign he didn't know what to do. Maybe it would be better to ask her in private. If she was going to shoot him down, he didn't want her doing it in front of their family.

"Hey, Len," Oz said, raising a glass that vaguely resembled multicolored cracked safety glass. "This reminds me of those mugs you tried to sell once."

Lena rolled her eyes at him, and her brother laughed.

"What's he talking about?" Elliot asked her.

Her cheeks blushed a gorgeous pink, and she shook her head. "Oh, nothing. Just one of my ideas that crashed and burned."

"Ideas?"

She shrugged. "Until Tyler started school, I stayed home with him, but I still wanted to help bring in some money, so Oz didn't have to work so hard."

"Mommy makes really cool stuff!"

Elliot's eyebrows rose. "Yeah? What kind of stuff?"

"She made me name letters for my room."

"Name letters?"

"Yeah, I got new ones this year. Soccer balls. I had dinosaurs for a while."

Elliot looked at Lena, totally lost. She pulled out her phone and scrolled through some pictures before holding it out for him to see. She had taken wood letters that spelled Tyler's name and painted them to look like soccer balls. She flicked to the next picture, and the name Brianna was decorated in pink and purple with sparkles and jewels and ribbons.

"Those are really cool."

She shrugged, but her shy smile showed she was pleased. "I have an Etsy store where I sell some crafty-type stuff. I'm always trying to bring in some extra cash. I keep hoping one of them will take off so I can get out of my generous brother's house," she said. "No luck so far."

"And one of the ideas was cracked glasses?" Elliot asked.

"No," she said with a little laugh. "I used to take this pottery class, and my instructor showed us how to make these really fun mugs. She had several shaped like dragons and trolls, really cool shapes. And I made one that turned out really well. I carved this pretty leaf design into it. It was nice."

"That sounds like a good idea. People love mugs. They always make great gifts."

She gave that little self-deprecating laugh again. "Yeah. That's what I thought. Problem was I had no idea how much all the equipment would cost. Plus, I didn't have a kiln or anything and firing them in my oven didn't quite work."

"Oh, no." He laughed.

"Yeah. I ended up with fifty cracked mugs that weren't good for much more than pencil holders. I sold a few at a craft fair...but not nearly enough to actually make a profit. Heck, even if they'd turned out great, I'd have had to make thousands of them to turn a profit. Not something I really had the time or resources to get going."

Before Elliot could say anything else, Tyler knocked over his water glass.

"Oh, Tyler! Shoot!" Lena jumped up before the water could trail down the table onto her lap.

Elliot slapped his napkin over the puddle and helped her get it mopped up. The waiter came over with more napkins, and in short order they had everything clean and dry. Elliot leaned over to draw her into conversation again, but Cherice got to her first. He thought about catching his sister's eye to give her the "go away" look, but wasn't sure that was such a good idea. Lena wasn't some random chick. She was Oz's sister, his own sister's soon to be in-law. He doubted Cherice would approve.

Then he caught the words "salon," "dress," and "nails" and sat back, any thought of butting-in gone. It sounded like they were talking shop for the wedding. There was no way he was going to attempt to interrupt a bride trying to iron out her wedding details. He'd seen *Bridezillas*. People had been stabbed for less.

He turned back to Tyler in time to see the boy wad up a

piece of napkin in his mouth and attempt to spit it through a straw. His face turned bright red but nothing came out the other end.

Elliot nudged him and picked up his own straw. "Watch," he said, ripping off a piece of napkin. He rolled it between his fingers. "It has to be small enough to fit through the straw. See?"

Then he popped it into his mouth and chewed until it was nice and juicy. "See that coconut up there?"

Tyler nodded, eyes huge with excitement. Elliot grabbed his straw and aimed at the fake tree next to their table. He took a deep breath and let it fly. The spitball splattered onto the coconut and stuck.

"Awesome!" Tyler cheered.

Cher and Lena looked over to see what the excitement was about. Lena's eyes narrowed. "Tyler Oserkowsi—"

Before she could really get into the scolding, Tyler piped up. "He did it!"

Elliot flushed. "Way to rat me out, kid."

Tyler shrugged.

Lena looked at him, her mouth opening and closing like she couldn't figure out what to say. Cher had no such problem.

"Seriously, Elliot? We're in a restaurant. And Tyler is watching everything you do. Don't teach him stuff like that."

"Sorry," Elliot muttered, though he glanced over at Tyler and gave him a quick wink.

Lena shook her head like she wasn't sure what to make of him and turned back to her conversation with Cher.

Tyler leaned over and whispered, "Hey, Elliot. Can I have your cookie?"

Elliot blinked down at the boy, not sure what he was talking about until he realized their dessert, some sort of sorbet with gourmet cookies sticking out of the dish, had been served. Damn. Dessert was his favorite course and not only had he not noticed it sitting there, but he had no real desire to eat it.

"Sure thing, little man. Here you go," he said, handing the little boy both his cookies.

"Yay, thanks!"

He started cramming them into his mouth as fast as he could. Elliot laughed. The kid looked like a little chipmunk with his cheeks bulging and crumbs spraying down his shirt.

"Tyler! No!"

Elliot blinked in surprise. Lena grabbed a napkin and held it under her son's chin. "Spit it out."

Elliot expected Tyler to argue, but he just stuck his tongue out, allowing all the crumbling goodness inside to spill out into his mother's hand.

"You've already had your dessert and half of mine. You eat anymore, and you're going to be up all night with a stomachache. Where did you get those cookies?"

Tyler pointed at Elliot. Lena turned to him with an exasperated sigh.

"Sorry," Elliot said with a sheepish grin.

At the rate he was going, he didn't need to worry about getting too close to the kid because Lena was never going to let him within two feet of Tyler again. The boy was already wired and slightly green around the gills from all the crap Elliot had let him eat. And here he was handing him more junk. "He asked."

"I know, but you can't always give kids everything they

ask for," she said, her reproach softened somewhat with a distracted smile. "He tends to gorge himself on any sugar source within a ten mile radius, but it doesn't sit well with him. Last time I let him eat too many cookies he puked all night. And with all the junk he ate earlier..." She trailed off and Elliot wondered if his face looked as guilty as he felt.

"Oh, wow. Sorry. Won't happen again."

Lena smiled again, but it wasn't an oh-he's-so-sweet smile, it was... It took Elliot a second to recognize it. It was the same smile his nanny had given him when he was growing up and had done something she disapproved of, for reasons he didn't understand. It was the mother look! Here he was, trying to impress her with his studliness, and she was looking at him like he was a misbehaving toddler. It was most definitely not the look a woman gave a man she was interested in.

New tactic. She'd appreciated his help earlier. He could be her knight in shining armor for the rest of the trip. After all, they were kind of stuck together for the week because of all the wedding stuff. Might as well be useful and possibly rack up a few brownie points while he was at it.

"So, have you spoken with your friend?" he asked. "Is she going to be able to make it?"

Lena's face fell. "I don't know. When I spoke with her earlier, the plane was stuck on the tarmac. She was supposed to text me when they finally took off, but that was a couple hours ago, and I still haven't heard from her. And when I checked the weather back there, it was getting worse, so it's not looking good. I'll call her in a bit and see what's going on."

"Oh, that's too bad. Well, if you need any help with Tyler,

I'd be more than happy to lend a hand."

She looked over Tyler's head at him and gave him a distracted nod. "Oh. Thanks, Elliot. That's very nice of you, but I think we'll be okay."

"Really, it'd be no trouble. Tyler and I had a great time this afternoon. I'd love to hang out some more. Maybe this time you could even hang out with us," he said, leaning forward and lowering his voice a notch.

He was finally rewarded with a faint blush, but she quickly looked down at her plate.

"We could go to the pool again, or the beach."

When she looked up in alarm, he hurried to assure her. "You wouldn't even have to get near the water. I could take Tyler for a swim, and you could soak up the rays on the beach."

"I'm not sure that's a great idea. Today was sort of a disaster. I don't want a repeat of that." She laughed, an embarrassed little giggle of a sound that wormed its way into his heart and took up residence.

"Well, this time I'd be there to protect you." He sent a little wink her way, and she blushed again but still shook her head.

"That's nice of you, really, but I still don't think it's a good idea."

Elliot caught sight of his sister's disapproving face at the head of the table and wrinkled his nose at her. She didn't approve of him hitting on her soon-to-be sister-in-law, he was sure, but he would have to reassure her later that he intended to be nothing but the perfect gentleman. He wanted to get to know Lena better. He wouldn't even mind spending some more time with Tyler. The kid was hilarious.

"It's no trouble, really. I'd love to hang out with you guys."

She was gearing up for another rejection, so he beat her to the punch. "If you'd rather not be near the water, there's lots of other stuff we can do."

"Can we play more video games?" Tyler asked, bouncing in his chair.

"Absolut—" Elliot almost agreed but glanced up at Lena in time.

"You've played enough video games for this trip, munchkin," she said. "There's too much other stuff to do than wasting your time playing video games."

She glanced up at him, her eyes wide and startled like she just realized he might take what she said as an insult. And he did. She was making it abundantly clear that she thought he was an immature screw-up who had no business being around her kid. And she was right. He generally was an immature screw-up, but it had never bothered him. Until that moment.

He didn't like that she didn't find him responsible enough to watch her son. Though, he honestly couldn't blame her. Remembering the scene she'd walked in on when she'd woken up made him want to squirm like he used to when he'd been Tyler's age and had gotten into stuff he shouldn't. Shit, he'd had the kid neck deep in junk food with a video game controller in one hand and a soda in the other. He should have known better. His only saving grace was that he'd at least chosen a semi-appropriate game and hadn't let the kid play something full of violent blood and gore. See? He wasn't totally clueless.

"No worries, little man," Elliot said, ruffling the kid's

hair. "We'll find something fun to do that Mommy will say yes to."

He winked at her over the top of Tyler's head. Her eyes narrowed in the classic mom glare, but those full, kissable lips of hers were smiling.

Now all he had to do was prove to her that he could be a responsible caretaker. Piece of cake.

L ena lounged back on the couch in her hotel room, surfing through the channels while Tyler snoozed in the bed nearby. The Goo Goo Doll's "Iris" rang from her phone, and Lena grabbed it from her pocket.

"Iris? Where are you? What's going on?"

Her friend groaned. "Still stuck in the damn airport."

"You're kidding? That's insane!"

"Tell me about it. First, the flight was delayed. Then when we finally got onto the damn plane, we sat on the tarmac for three hours. Three hours in that little tin can. I was about ready to chew my way out before they finally pulled back into the gate and let us off. Now we're just sitting here."

"Do they know when you'll get to leave?"

"They said nine tomorrow morning is the earliest flight I can get out. The snow is coming down so hard you can't even see out the window."

"Oh my God, that sucks."

"You have no idea. You should see this place. There are bodies littered everywhere. The airlines have cots and stuff set up in case people want to sleep."

"You're kidding? What happened to getting you a hotel

room?"

"Apparently they can't afford to set up dozens of flights' worth of passengers in cheap motels. So it looks like I'm stuck here unless I want to go get my own hotel. I'll probably try, but I'm not sure how much transportation is running right now."

"Wonderful," Lena groaned.

"Hey, what are you grumbling for? I'm the one stuck in this frozen pit. You're the lucky shit who's lying on a beach in the tropics."

Lena snorted and Iris laughed. "Okay, so maybe not."

"Well, I did actually take Tyler to the pool today."

"You did *not*! Good for you."

"Yeah, don't be all proud of me yet. I had a total panic attack when I couldn't get him out of the pool and I fainted."

"Oh my God." Iris laughed. "I'm not laughing," she said, laughing harder. "But oh my God."

"Yeah. It was fantastic. Fell right into the arms of my brother's new brother-in-law."

"*Oooh*. Well that sounds interesting, at least. Is he gorgeous, or did Cher get all the looks in the family?"

Lena's stomach did a queer little flip-flop. "Oh, the family is definitely blessed, that's for sure. Looks-wise at least."

"*Hmm*, what does that mean?"

Lena sighed. "Nothing. Elliot is perfectly charming. He was great with Tyler. Obviously knows nothing at all about kids. But they had fun playing together."

Iris laughed. "Ah. Total man-child, eh?"

"Completely."

"Well, no law saying you can't have fun with the guy while you're out there."

"Iris!"

"What? Someone's gotta have fun. It sure as hell won't be me."

"*Ugh*. I'm sorry you're stuck there."

"Me, too. So much for helping you out. Hopefully, I can get out of here tomorrow so I can actually keep Tyler out of your hair."

"I feel so bad," Lena said, rubbing her forehead. "They have these amazing pools and mini-water parks. He wants to play in them so bad. I just can't…Elliot offered but…"

"Well, hell woman! If Mr. Stud Man is offering, why not take him up on it?"

"First of all, I'm not sure I trust Tyler with him. Elliot is sweet and all, but he *is* completely clueless about kids. He'd be letting him swim in the deep end and go down the scary water tubes. And I'm sure sunscreen would never even occur to him."

"Oh my God, he sounds like a monster. Someone call the cops."

"Oh, shut up," Lena said, though she couldn't keep the grin from spreading over her face. Yeah, she knew she was a little overprotective. But even if she wasn't, Elliot was hardly someone who was even remotely qualified to be a babysitter.

"Besides, you know how Tyler gets. He's already talking about Elliot constantly, and he only spent an hour with him. He gets attached to men so easily."

"Yeah, I know. Well, with any luck this damn snow will let up and I can be on my way. I am so ready for a little tropical relaxation."

"I bet. I hope you get out of there soon."

"Yeah, me, too—wait a minute. Well, hello there…"

"What?"

"Things might be looking up," Iris said, her voice sounding like she had her mouth pressed to the phone, trying to be quiet.

"Why's that?"

"There was this totally hot cowboy on the plane sitting behind me. We tried to talk, but it was hard not being in the same row."

"Okay…"

"He just sat down across from me. And he looks even better up close than he did crammed into those little airplane seats. I can see a whole lot more of him now. Hat, boots, and incredibly tight jeans that are leaving very little to my imagination, if you know what I mean."

"I can guess."

"I think I'm going to go make friends."

Lena laughed. She wished she could be as outgoing and adventurous as Iris. "Don't have too much fun."

"Hell, I might be stuck in this airport for the rest of the night. A girl's gotta keep herself entertained somehow. If you were smart, you'd find yourself a little entertainment, too."

"Yeah, I don't think so."

"Seriously, babe. Not every relationship has to go somewhere. You can have some fun. You're in a tropical paradise. Take Tyler to the hotel day care and go have yourself a good time. You'll feel a 1,000 percent better."

"I'll keep that in mind."

"You do that. Call me later."

"I will," Lena said.

Iris was saying hi to her cowboy before she'd even ended

the call.

Lena put the phone onto the table, her mind turning over what Iris had said. The memory of Elliot's rock solid body rising out of the pool, water streaming over the lines of his muscles, made her belly tighten and heat up in places she usually tried very hard to ignore. It had been a very, very long time since she'd "had a good time" as Iris had put it, with any man.

She'd tried dating a few times, but she hadn't found anyone worth spending what little free time she had. And with Tyler's tendency to latch on to any friendly male face, Lena was incredibly careful who she introduced him to. There had only been one boyfriend, actually, that Lena had thought might make the cut. And when it hadn't worked out, Tyler had been more crushed than she had. There was no way she'd let that happen again.

Sure, she could probably have a harmless hookup. But… Well, she'd never done that before and didn't even know how to go about it. Having a good time wasn't as easy as Iris made it seem. Especially when the man in question was going to be her brother's brother-in-law. Which meant they'd probably see each other now and then. Which meant *awkward*. Which meant absolutely no hookup. Which really kind of sucked. Elliot, with his laughing eyes, absolutely gorgeous body, and fun, carefree attitude, would have been perfect.

Too dangerous, though. A girl could get addicted to a guy like Elliot. And even if her circumstances were different, Elliot didn't seem the type to be into long term, monogamous relationships, with a single mom, no less. Which meant he was off-limits.

Damn it.

Chapter Four

Elliot fumed, but arguing with his parents wasn't going to make the situation better. He'd pulled them aside to talk to them about his goal of doubling the funds he brought in for the charity. And while they were on board with that, it hadn't been enough to really impress them and prove that he was capable of running the children's charity on his own.

His mother stood to leave first. "I'm happy to see you making some sort of effort, Elliot. And increased funds would, of course, be welcomed."

"But it's going to take more than that to prove to us you're serious about your role in this charity," his father added. "I agree with your mother that this renewed interest from you is a good thing. But you'll have to forgive us if we don't put much faith in how long it will last."

Elliot bit his tongue again. That was the crux of it right there. He couldn't argue. He hadn't ever shown much interest in truly running the charity and the few times he had hadn't lasted long. So how in the hell was he supposed to convince them he meant it *now*?

His mother patted his cheek as she walked by. His father stopped in front of him, sizing him up. "The last thing I want to do is discourage you from finally stepping up. But this charity is too important to let you continue to ignore your responsibility. If you can come up with an idea, something concrete, I'll think about it. But for now…"

He left it at that and escorted Elliot's mom from the dining room. Elliot gave them enough time to be gone from the hallway before marching out. So… He needed to come up with something better, more concrete, and soon. Or he'd be leaving the island and going home to the same old, same old. He couldn't blame them for their stance, but that didn't mean he liked it. The thought of being demoted on the board sent a wave of anxiety through him that was strong enough to make him nauseous. The charity was the only thing of any substance in his life. He wanted to truly make it his.

The sound of children's laughter made him pause. He glanced in the windows of the big double doors he'd been passing and realized he was standing in front of the hotel's day care center. He took a closer look. Damn. It would be fun to be a kid again if he could hang out in that place. It looked like a McDonald's Playland on crack. Cleaner and more organized, maybe. But just as fun.

Then he saw something even better. Lena. Saying good-bye to Tyler. She must have decided to get a little alone time, after all. And he happened to be right here. It was fate. Hanging out with her would definitely cheer him up, if he could convince her to tolerate his presence for a few minutes. With that idea-centric brain of hers, she might even help him come up with something good enough to convince his parents to let him rejuvenate the charity.

Hopefully, she wouldn't shoot him down the second she walked out the door. He'd never had to work this hard to get a woman's attention. But there was something about the way she looked at him. She was interested. She was just trying to ignore it. He knew the feeling. But he couldn't seem to ignore her.

Lena gave Tyler one last hug and started for the door. Elliot hurried over to stand on the opposite side of the hallway. Didn't want to look like he'd been totally stalking.

She breezed through the door, and Elliot froze for a second, captivated by the sheer beauty of her. The couple times he'd seen her after the pool incident, she'd been tense and on edge. But now she almost bounced down the hallway with a naturally carefree gait that he loved. Her honey blond hair was twisted into a messy bun on the back of her head, and as far as he could tell, she wore no makeup other than a hint of mascara on her long lashes. Her sleeveless maxi dress left her toned arms bare to the sun, and when she lifted the hem to hop up the few stairs that would bring her into his part of the hallway, he got a delicious view of spectacularly muscled calves. She worked out. Or maybe it was from chasing Tyler around. That had to be a workout all on its own.

Whatever she did, it showed. She was natural, easy going, and totally unpretentious and somehow managed to be incredibly sexy even with that damn fanny pack around her waist. It was refreshing. Her cornflower blue eyes sparkled. The exact opposite of everything he usually found attractive.

His girlfriends ran more to the overly made up, designer, high maintenance end of the spectrum. And they generally tended to *want* him. Or at least his connections. Not something Lena apparently suffered from. For the thousandth time, he wondered why he didn't go find some other woman who would be happy to hook up with him. But Lena was *different*. That's what he was looking for.

She glanced up and caught his gaze. Her face lit up at the sight of him, and all his concerns flew right out the window. The happiness to see him lasted only a second before she seemed to remember she wasn't supposed to be interested, but that moment was more than enough encouragement for him.

"Hey there," he said, giving her the full Debusshere charm.

She smiled but her eyes skittered away, no longer meeting his gaze.

He wasn't going to give her a chance to vanish on him. He started talking before she had a chance to make an excuse to leave. "So I guess your friend won't be making it, after all?" he said, nodding toward the day care doors.

"No. Thank God the hotel has a day care center."

"Definitely a plus," he said, pleased. "I was hoping I'd run into you. I found this great spot I think you'll really love."

She hesitated. "Oh, that sounds fun but…"

"Don't worry. It's not near any water."

She blushed and his heart rate kicked up a notch. She opened her mouth to object again, but Elliot pressed on. "I was actually hoping I could pick your brain a bit."

Her eyes widened in what he hoped was interest.

"About what?" she asked.

He took her hand and drew her along with him. She didn't pull away, and he resisted the urge to fist bump the air. He wasn't free and clear yet. But she hadn't run screaming down the hallway, either. That was a good sign.

"Well, I was thinking about all those cool ideas you've had."

Lena blushed again. "Most of them aren't worth anything. I mean, I think the concepts are good. Some of them, anyway. But either I have no way of actually getting things going or I come across some other issue. Nothing has panned out."

"*Hmm*, well I might be able to help in that department. And I'm hoping you might be able to help me."

A delicate blond eyebrow arched. "I don't see how. I might have good ideas, but like I said, they never go anywhere. A good idea doesn't mean much if you can't follow it through."

Elliot scoffed. "Don't underestimate yourself. Maybe you just haven't found the right business partner."

The other eyebrow joined the first. Before she could say anything else, Elliot stopped.

"What do you think?"

She glanced around at the lush paradise surrounding them, her eyes widening the more she took in. Her mouth dropped open to form a little *O*, and happy pleasure zinged through Elliot. He'd done well.

"What is this place?"

"I found it last night when I was wandering around after dinner. The concierge said there are several of them hidden away around the resort."

"It's gorgeous. Really. Just incredible."

Elliot was beaming like a fool, but he couldn't help it. Being the one who put that amazing smile on her face gave him a buzz like nothing he'd ever experienced before.

He led her deeper into the small botanical garden. Opulent plants and flowers crowded all around them, small paths strung with twinkle lights zigzagged throughout. Exotic birds perched in a few of the trees, their song following them. Elliot led Lena into the heart of the lush mini-jungle where a few lounge chairs were set up. Two other guests lazed around, but for the most part, they had the place to themselves. Elliot ordered a couple drinks from a passing waiter, and within a few minutes, they were sipping on two very large tropical cocktails.

Thin pipes were camouflaged within the trees, and every few minutes they'd release a fine mist of water that was enough to cool without soaking the guests. Lena jumped when the mist first fell with a faint hiss, but then she turned her face up to catch the coolness with delighted pleasure.

"Is this okay?" he asked, though by the look on her face she was enjoying it.

She gave a little laugh. "Yes. It's only bodies of water that make me a little nervous. Rain, showers, that kind of thing, don't bother me."

He could envision her standing in a shower all too easily and tried to steer clear of that particular distraction. He wanted to get to know her a little better, get her comfortable with him. Not pant after her like some horny teenager.

He led her over to the chairs and sat down next to her. Lena leaned back on her chaise with a happy sigh. "Okay, *this* I could get used to."

Elliot took a healthy slug of his own drink and settled back. "Don't get to relax much?"

She laughed. "Not often, no. Between Tyler and work, I think the last time I just sat down and did nothing was…"

A small frown formed between her brows. "Huh. I honestly don't remember."

"That's something that should definitely be remedied."

She laughed again. "That would be nice. I'll let my boss know."

"What do you do?"

"I'm an office aide at Tyler's school. It's great because I work the same schedule that he's in school. But I'm surrounded by kids all day, which can get…overwhelming sometimes. This break is nice."

"I bet. Well, if one of your business ideas takes off, you can spend all your time on a lounge chair and hire people to do everything else for you."

Lena snorted. "That would be nice. Honestly, I would just love for me and Tyler to be able to get our own place, not have to rely on my brother so much. When I had Tyler, Oz helped out so I could stay home with him. It was actually cheaper than working and putting him in day care. Now that he's in school, I'm willing to do anything, but my resume isn't the most impressive. I like working at the school, but I still can't afford to get us on our own. And there's not much else I can do, though I've applied at enough places. If I could make enough money with one of these ideas… But like I said, my plans seem to be great in concept only."

Elliot inwardly cringed at the rush of shame that hit him. It had never occurred to him how hard it might be for people to find jobs. He'd always assumed if people really wanted to work, they just needed to go out and do it.

From what he'd heard from Cher and Oz, Lena definitely had the brains to develop something that could really be successful. But there was more to making a profit in business than just having a good idea. Maybe that was some way he could help.

"I'm sure your ideas are better than you think. Tell me some."

She waved her hand like she was trying to erase his words from the air. "You don't want to hear those."

"No, I really do. Come on. I've heard a couple of them already."

"What? From who?"

"Cherice told me a few."

Lena blinked, surprised. "She did? Why?"

"She was impressed with them."

She snorted again, a sound that Elliot normally found irritating in other people. But Lena's snort was a delicate sort of poof of air that sounded more like a wheeze than an actual snort. It was adorable.

"I doubt that. They've all been disasters."

"Oh, come on. I'm sure they weren't all that bad."

"Really? You've already heard about the mug fiasco."

Elliot laughed. "Yeah, but that wasn't a bad idea. If you'd had the manpower and the right equipment, you might have made a go of it."

"Maybe," she said, but she didn't look convinced.

"Come on. Tell me the worst idea you've ever had."

"The worst?"

"Yeah. Get that one out of the way, and then we can go from there."

She shook her head. "The worst was another mug idea. After the baked pottery ones fell through, I thought about making some out of stained glass. We were sitting in a church for a friend's wedding one day, and I was staring at the windows, thinking how wonderful it would be to wake up to that view every morning. With an enclosed back porch or kitchen window or something with stained glass that I could enjoy while I sipped my coffee."

"That does sound amazing."

"Right? Well, then I thought instead of a porch or window, which I'd never be able to do, why not make the mugs out of stained glass. There are clear glass mugs, so I figured stained glass wouldn't be that much harder."

"Makes sense. I think it's a great idea. They'd be gorgeous."

"That's what I thought. Until I talked to a glass blower."

"And?"

"She laughed me out of the building."

"Why?"

"Because stained glass has those little veins of lead running through it to keep the different panes of glass separate."

"And…"

"She didn't think it would be a great idea to give customers lead poisoning."

Elliot's eyes widened, and he barked a laugh. "I didn't even think about that. Well, damn. But it was a good idea."

"Yeah, but apparently not all good ideas are actually marketable."

He laughed again. "Apparently."

"The one that came the closest to actually making some money was my gift baskets."

"Gift baskets?"

She took a sip of her drink and nodded. "I wanted to get a gift basket for one of my co-workers for her birthday one year. Went online to check out prices, and they were insane! I'm talking sixty dollars for a tiny basket that probably cost ten dollars to put together. If that. And then they tacked shipping and delivery fees on to it. So I figured if all those businesses could make money charging outrageous prices, I could make something just as good, and probably better, charge less, and still make a good profit."

"Sounds like a great plan. So why didn't that one work out?"

Lena shrugged again. "It did okay. I always sold the baskets I made, but I ended up having to severely drop my prices to do it. I guess when you are a new business, it's hard to get noticed unless you are selling for peanuts. I sold what I made, but I was only making a few dollars profit per basket, and I wasn't getting many large orders for multiple baskets or for the high-end gourmet ones. I sold at a few fairs, but for those I had to buy all the materials ahead of time, and I didn't always have the cash on hand to take a really good selection. If I'd had more time or money, more marketing, help. Maybe…"

Elliot was impressed. "Well, maybe I can help you there."

"What do you mean?" she asked, her eyes watching him warily.

"I might not be great with ideas, but marketing and fundraising I can do. Apparently, it's about the only thing I can do." He injected the words with as much humor as he could to hide how much the reality stung.

"That's sweet of you, but you don't have to do that," she said.

"I want to. It would be my pleasure to help you out."

She shook her head, her lips pressed together. "I can do it on my own. But thanks."

Elliot left it alone for the moment. He couldn't force

her to accept his help. But he could do his best to persuade her. Carefully, though, so she didn't bolt on him with his first suggestion.

"You know, every idea I've heard from you, whether it's worked or not, has been great. I haven't heard one crazy idea yet. They're good. You've definitely got a mind for this."

Lena blushed and focused her attention on her drink. "That's nice of you to say."

Elliot leaned over and put his finger under her chin, raising her eyes to meet his. "I'm not just trying to be nice. I mean every word."

She didn't move away from his touch. He let his hand linger on her face while her gaze searched his. Whatever she saw must have made her happy because a bright, sweet smile spread across her face. He ran his tongue over his suddenly dry lips. He wanted nothing more than to close the few inches between them and capture that mouth with his. Her own mouth dropped open a little.

Elliot leaned forward, his hand gently trailing from her chin down the slender column of her neck. His heart thundered in his chest, a tangle of desire tightening low in his belly. He didn't think he'd ever wanted anything so badly in his whole life as he wanted to kiss her.

Lena blinked, sucked in a quick breath, and pulled out of his reach. She fumbled with her drink, her cheeks flaming so hotly he was tempted to dig an ice cube out of his glass to see if it would melt on her skin.

She put her drink down and stood up. Elliot followed, hoping she wasn't trying to make a break for it already. Things were going great. He was really enjoying talking to her.

"You want to walk for a minute?" she asked.

He breathed a sigh of relief. "Sure." He offered her his arm, surprised when, after a brief moment of hesitation, she actually took it. He pulled her in as close as he thought he could get away with. Her faint coconut scent washed over him, and he inhaled deeply. God, she smelled good. Good enough to taste.

They wandered through the gardens for a few minutes, stopping every now and then to look at some exotic plant or another. The more they walked, the more relaxed she seemed. She kept hold of his arm, even drawing closer to him a few times. A faint hope that she'd follow through with her interest in him blossomed in his chest.

"So, you said you wanted to get some ideas from me. For what?" she asked.

A small bench was set back under some trees, and he drew her over so they could sit in the shade.

"I run my family's charity. It does well, but I think it could do much better."

"What kind of charity?"

"Well, that's part of the problem. Right now, it's kind of a general Help-the-Poor-Children-type charity. But we don't do much with it. Every year we hold a big fundraiser, and we usually have a great turn out and make decent money, but then the money gets spread out to so many different organizations I'm not sure how much good it's doing. I feel we need to focus it more. Make it bigger, better. Turn it into a foundation that can really do some good."

"That sounds amazing. What do your parents think?"

Elliot scowled, his frustration with his family dampening his good mood. "They think things are fine as they are. The charity is making money for good causes, and they don't really have to think about it much. That's how they like it."

"Surely they can see how much better it would do if it was expanded. Even if they are only doing it to look good, having a successful charity be even more successful would be nothing but good press for them."

Elliot laughed. "I've never put it to them like that. I'll have to lead with that argument next time. The main problem is getting them to listen. They don't see the need to change anything, so they don't even want to listen to my ideas. And to be honest, I haven't always been as involved as I should be, so throwing ideas out at them with no real plan won't work. Now, if it was Lilah with the ideas, this wouldn't be an issue at all."

"Lilah is your older sister, right?"

Elliot nodded. "She's always been the golden child. Followed in Dad's medical footsteps. Cherice is more like me. Fitting, I guess, since we're twins. Mom and Dad have never really approved of her and her disadvantaged women's boutique. But she didn't care. Actually, I think your brother helped a lot there."

"How?" Lena asked.

"Cherice was already kind of the black sheep, moving off to North Carolina, ignoring our parents' wishes when it came to her job. But she didn't really jump off the deep end and commit to what she wanted to do with her shop and everything until she met Oz."

Lena nodded thoughtfully, her face softening at the mention of her brother. Elliot stared at her, wondering what it was about the Oserkowskis that seemed to inspire the Debussheres. There must be something there because his sister had completely upended her life and was about to march up the aisle to marry a mechanic turned aspiring journalist who had no prestigious ties anywhere in his family tree. And Elliot… He'd been thinking of making some major changes, yes, but Lena seemed to be lighting the fire under him to actually *do* it.

Lena's forehead crinkled in thought. "Okay. So, why don't you approach this differently?"

"What do you mean?"

"Instead of coming to them as their son with an idea for the family charity, approach them as the president of a charitable foundation, complete with a fully developed business plan or presentation. Make an appointment to see them with their assistants, if you need to. Show them you are serious, and they might take you a little more seriously."

Wow. She didn't pull any punches. If he didn't know better, he'd swear he was in danger of blushing.

"I know I'm not really the kind of guy that most people take seriously. I guess I shouldn't expect my parents to be any different."

Lena's eyes flared wide, and she shook her head, putting her hand onto his knee. "No, that's not what I meant at all."

Elliot froze, afraid if he made any sudden movements she'd remove her hand. He was beyond thankful that his resort-wear tastes leaned heavily on the beach bum look. Her hand rested on the bare skin of his knee, not an area he'd ever thought of as erogenous, but there now seemed to be a direct line of fire from his kneecap straight to his groin. If she gripped or rubbed his knee one more time, he would need to find more comfortable accommodations for his favorite body part.

She removed her hand, and he wasn't sure whether to sigh in relief or beg her to put it back.

She was still apologizing, and he'd totally forgotten why. Oh! She thought she'd insulted him about the whole serious guy thing. Right.

"It's okay, Lena," he said, interrupting her. "I like to have fun. No point in being miserable, but when the occasion calls for it, I can get the job done. Of course, my parents don't seem to think so. I think that might be why they keep shooting me down. I mean, expanding a charity is hardly a *bad* thing to do. But if they think it'll be more work for them, they'll oppose it."

"Exactly. So you need to go in fully prepared to answer all their questions and show them you *are* serious about it."

"Right."

"So, first you need a rock solid idea."

Elliot frowned. "Where do I get one of those?"

Lena laughed and the sound washed over him like the cool ocean spray—refreshing, invigorating, and completely addicting. He had the irresistible urge to make it his mission in life to make the woman in front of him laugh as often as possible.

"I'm not sure I'm the best one to help you with this. It's obviously important to you. I'm kind of bad luck when it comes to business stuff."

"I don't believe in bad luck."

She snorted. "Wait a while. We've just met. You hang around me long enough, and you'll believe, trust me."

He laughed. "Oh, come on. I'm sure if we put our heads together, we can do amazing things."

Lena's gaze flashed to his, and he let his lips stretch into a sexy grin. She bit her lip and looked down, a slight blush staining her cheeks. Good. She'd caught that little innuendo. The fact that he could affect her like that with only a few words sent a rush of adrenaline through him. What was she doing to him? The weird hyper-focus he had on her should scare the shit out of him. But it didn't. Instead, it made him even more determined to get as close to her as possible.

She looked up to find him still staring at her. Caught red-handed, he had no shame. He kept right on staring. Her cheeks flamed hotter, but she didn't look away. A smile to match his graced her amazing, full lips. Elliot's breath hitched in his throat, and her smile stretched wider.

"Well. Let's see what we can come up with then," she said.

Elliot held out his hand. She hesitated for a second and then slipped her hand into his. It felt so small wrapped in his. Tiny, soft. But strong. Just like Lena.

He shook his head, a little startled at the thoughts running rampant in his mind. If he wasn't careful, he was going to fall for her. Shouldn't that thought send him screaming for the hills?

Somewhere during her conversation with Elliot, Lena realized she was having a good time. A really good time. Apparently, there was a lot more to Elliot than a gorgeous face and a body to drool for. In fact, despite the whole man-child act, he was surprisingly intelligent. Just thinking that made Lena cringe.

She once had a school buddy who had been totally

shocked when report cards came out and Lena had straight *A*s, because, according to the friend, Lena came off as a total airhead. That had stung. She liked to laugh and amuse people, but that didn't mean she was a ditz. No more than Elliot liking to have a good time and not knowing anything about kids made him some immature party boy.

She stamped down the urge to apologize to him. The guilt at her snap judgment sat like an uncomfortable knot in her stomach. She redoubled her efforts to help him with his ideas.

They'd wandered back to the lounge chairs, and she sat on the edge of one before crossing her legs and facing him.

"So, you said you wanted to expand your parents' charity, keep doing something with children, but more focused?"

His face lit up. "Yes. I know we could do so much more than we are doing now. Which is where I was hoping you'd come in."

"Me, with all my great business ideas, huh?"

"Stop with the tone," he chided, narrowing his eyes at her.

She smiled. Kind of hard not to when a guy who should be gracing the cover of some Sexiest Men magazine was staring down at her like a disapproving school marm.

"Sorry. I'll try to keep all tone to a minimum."

"See that you do," he said with a little mock glower that had her stomach doing happy cartwheels. "Now, back to what I was saying. Yes, you with all your great ideas. Look, they might not have panned out, but you definitely have a knack for thinking outside the box. For seeing something that I wouldn't even notice and turning it into this great possible 'something.' That's what I need. A little spark of what you've got going on up here."

He reached up and touched her temple, letting his finger linger to make his point. When he dropped his hand, his finger trailed down her skin for a second, but it was enough to make goose bumps erupt on that side of her body.

She realized she was sitting frozen, staring into his amber eyes. She tore her gaze away and looked down at her hands. "Well, I don't know. Do you want me to start throwing ideas out there?"

"Yes," he said, leaning back onto the chaise with his hands behind his head. "Throw away."

Lena laughed. "Okay. Well, do you have a particular group of kids you want to help?"

"I know there are a lot of kids that need helping, but I'd like to do something that isn't being done yet. I think I'd actually like to do something with foster kids. Maybe sponsor a summer camp. Or give them some sort of gift basket or care package when they move to a new home."

"You know, that's not a bad idea."

"Really?"

The surprise on his face was beyond adorable. Lena fought to keep her mind on the topic at hand. "Really. I mean, not a gift basket."

"No," Elliot continued. "But something similar. Foster kids usually don't have much, if anything, as they move from home to home. Some kids only have a trash bag to haul whatever belongings they might have with them. And many of them first coming into the system have nothing at all."

"That's terrible."

Elliot nodded. "So what can we do to fix that?"

Lena's heart skipped a beat or two at the word "we."

She pressed on, the familiar excitement rushing through her with the onset of a new idea. "What if we took your care package idea but expanded it?" She sat forward, her hands starting to fly as she spoke. "You could coordinate with whoever is in charge of placing the children in homes, and when someone new enters the system, you can do something special for them."

Elliot sat up, his intent gaze totally focused on her. "I love that idea. We can give them something of their own. They'd have their own things to take into a new home. That would not only give them their own stuff but would help out the foster parents as well, so they wouldn't need to provide so much."

"Yes! What if we got something like those large plastic bins? We could decorate them pretty, put the child's name on it, and fill it with everything they'll need."

Elliot nodded. "Exactly. Like sheets, clothing, books, toys. Even toiletry items, brushes, toothpaste. So that when they go to their first foster home, and if they have to move to others, they've got their very own things to take with them, in a case that's theirs alone."

"That would be perfect!"

He grabbed her hands and pulled her into a quick hug. "It is. It's simple, but something those kids really need and would love. And it wouldn't cost much for each child, so we'd be able to stretch the money further. We could even get the community involved. People could sponsor a child. Volunteer to create the case and fill it with items. This is so good. Really."

"It is!"

Elliot stood up and pulled her to her feet, yanking her in

for another hug. This time it lasted a little longer. He let her go a little slower. Her excitement for their idea died away, replaced by a very different kind of thrill running through her. One she hadn't felt in a very long time.

She looked up, met his gaze while his arms were still draped loosely around her. It would be so easy to lean in a bit, press the rest of her body to his, rise up onto her toes, and close the distance between their mouths.

Elliot leaned down a little, as if his thoughts mirrored her own. She knew she shouldn't. But… One little kiss wouldn't hurt…

She moved enough for her lips to brush his. He jerked a little in surprise but recovered quickly, tightening his hold on her to keep her against him. His mouth moved over hers with increased intensity.

Oh my God.

Lena trembled and pressed herself closer, every nerve in her body blazing in a flood of heat that left her head swimming.

Her watch alarm went off, and she jumped with a little squeak, her heart pounding in her chest. She slapped at the thing until she connected with the button that shut it off. Elliot laughed, but he didn't let her go. He held her lightly enough that she could pull away if she wanted, giving her the choice.

She almost hated to make it, but she knew it was the smart thing to do. She drew away from him, but smiled to take the sting out of any rejection he might feel.

"I need to go pick up Tyler."

"Ah. Well. May I escort you back?"

She looked back into those shining, eager eyes. How he

managed to both make her want to laugh like a total goof-ball and shove him up against the wall with her tongue down his throat, all at the same time, was beyond her. Just talent-ed, she supposed. And she knew she should say no. Business talk was all well and good, but more than that could be bad.

Then again, hell, it was just a walk, and she actually didn't know where she was, so…

"Sure. I'd like that."

Lena shoved the responsible-mommy part of her that was sending up warning flares and SOS signals down into some deep, dark box that she could ignore for at least a few more minutes.

Elliot reached out and took her hand, his brow lifting in a brief question. She should pull away. Her momentary lapse in judgment was already coming back to bite her in the ass. Because all she wanted to do was finish what they'd started. That small taste hadn't been nearly enough. And if one tiny kiss could affect her this much, then anything more would be a colossal mistake. She should walk, no *run*, away.

Instead, she curled her fingers around his and tried to keep from taking his hand and rubbing her cheek over it like a cat scent-marking its territory. His thumb lightly caressed her skin as they walked. Each stroke was like adding a new butterfly to the mix already cascading through her stomach, fluttering uncontrollably at the mere touch of his skin brush-ing hers.

Good God, if she was finding it difficult to do normal things like breathe and hold a coherent thought in her head just because he held her hand, she could only imagine what it would feel like if he touched other parts of her. Bare skin to bare skin. She inhaled so quickly at the fantasy images flooding her head that it came out in a soft gasp, and Elliot looked down at her.

"You okay?"

"Yeah, fine." Except for her cheeks, which were filling with enough blood to make her light-headed. "Must have swallowed a bug or something."

Elliot grimaced. "I hope it was a mosquito. The damn things have been eating me alive."

She grinned. "Me, too. Actually, here." She stopped and reluctantly pulled her hand from his so she could dig around in her fanny pack.

Elliot peered into the recesses of the bag, eyes narrowed.

"What?" she asked, pulling out a small tin container.

"I've been meaning to ask why you carry that thing. What could possibly be important enough that you need to strap that monstrosity onto your body?"

From someone else, that might have hurt her feelings. But there was no malice in Elliot. He might be poking a little fun, but somehow he exuded enough good will that you could tell he was having fun with you, not at you. There was a huge difference. And besides, she was well aware of how unfashionable the Mommy Pack was, as Tyler called it.

She held up the tin. "So I always have stuff like this on hand, for one. I have a kid. I used to carry around a purse large enough to pack half our house in. Okay, I still carry that thing around, but for trips such as these, the pack works great. I've got baby wipes, hand sanitizer, sunscreen, tissues, a little bottle of water, tweezers... Well, you get the point. It's always better to be prepared."

Elliot was laughing, though his eyes looked slightly glazed over. "And what is that stuff?" he asked, pointing at the tin she was opening.

She scooped a little of the ointment onto her finger. "Bug bite remedy."

"You made this?" He took the tin from her and sniffed it.

"*Mmm-hmm.* Just some coconut oil, a little olive oil, and some other essential oils. Works better than any store stuff I've found."

"It actually smells pretty good. You sure this won't make them eat me more?"

She laughed. "No, I promise. Now where does it itch?"

He pointed to a few spots on his arms, and she applied the balm to the bites, taking her time as she did so. Not so slow that she was being obvious about it. She hoped. But long enough to enjoy the feel of his skin and the muscles beneath it. Such an intoxicating mix of soft and hard. She wondered how that skin would feel beneath her lips. She leaned closer. Her mouth actually parted slightly, like she would quickly lean forward and take a tiny taste.

She caught herself in time, before she did anything too humiliating. Barely.

She started to pull away, but Elliot's voice stopped her. "You missed one."

Lena glanced up. Elliot's gaze burned into hers, and he closed the already small distance between them so she was nearly pressed against his body.

Her breath hitched, but she tried to force herself to breathe normally.

"Where?" she said, though it was more a whisper than an actual word.

He pointed to a spot on his neck, just under his ear. She

scooped a little more ointment out, and he leaned down so she could get to the bite. It put his face mere inches from hers, their breath mingling together while she tended to the bite. She rubbed the balm on it for much longer than necessary.

Elliot reached up and took her hand. She tried to pull away, heat burning her cheeks. But he didn't let her. Instead, he pulled her even closer. Her startled eyes met his. He moved slowly enough that she could back away if she wanted. But she didn't. Sweet Mother of all that was holy, she was very happy to stay right where she was. The responsible wench having a shit fit in her head could shut the hell up. No way was Lena turning this down.

Elliot smiled against her lips and whispered, "Thank you."

She had half a second to wonder if he was thanking her for the bite balm or for letting him kiss her before his lips covered hers. It started gently, just a sweet kiss, a bare brush of his lips on hers. Even that small touch had sparks shooting through her, jump starting her heart. Then his hand came up to cup her face, his fingers threading into her hair, and he pulled her in closer, his lips increasing the pressure, moving with hers. His other hand tightened around her waist, drawing her in as close to him as she could get.

She leaned into him. His rock hard chest beneath her softer curves made her want to rub against him like a cat against a bedpost. If he kept up the magic his lips were working she'd be purring too. Her wrists trailed up his arms. She still held the bite balm, but she had no intention of breaking the kiss to put it away. She'd make do.

His lips parted, and he kissed her again, tilting his head

for a better angle. His tongue flicked against her lips, and she opened for him, sucking in a sharp breath that ended on a quiet moan in the back of her throat. The noise spurred him on, and he crushed her to him, exploring every corner of her mouth, their lips moving together, tasting each other like they'd never get enough. Her heart raced, every nerve ending tingling. She wrapped her arms around his neck, rising onto her toes so she could get closer.

It was a good thing he was holding on to her because she'd fall over if he let go. She'd read about the whole light-headed feeling in her romance novels, even had a friend tell her that's how she'd felt the first time she'd kissed her husband. But Lena had never had someone kiss her until her toes curled and she got dizzy. Either it had been too long since she'd been kissed or he was just that damn good.

Elliot came up for air, tilted his head in the other direction, and dragged her back to his lips with both hands cupping her face. Lena moaned again. Oh yeah. He was that good.

Tap, tap, tap.

Giggles erupted and someone tapped on the glass again. Lena gasped and jerked herself out of Elliot's arms. She hadn't realized they'd come to a stop right in front of the day care center doors and half a dozen little faces were smiling up at them from behind the window set in the door.

Heat flooded her face, and she took another step away from Elliot, sending up a quick prayer of thanks to whoever was listening that Tyler wasn't one of the kids who'd seen them.

She shoved the bite balm back into her fanny pack and tucked her hair behind her ear. She found it hard to meet

Elliot's gaze again. Now why would that be? *Hmm,* maybe because she'd been making out like a teenager in front of a room full of preschoolers. Smooth. Very smooth.

"Thank you," Elliot said again.

Lena glanced up at him, wondering for the second time what exactly he was thanking her for. Because if it was for the kiss, he was stealing her line. Hell, she was seriously considering buying him a card, engraved with fancy calligraphy, the whole nine yards. That hadn't been a mere kiss. That had been… She had no words to even describe it.

"For all the ideas on the foundation," he said, though the heat lingering in his eyes suggested that wasn't all he was happy with.

She hoped he was just a good mind reader and that she hadn't actually said any of that out loud. As flustered as she was at the moment, it was a good possibility.

"You're welcome." Her voice came out steady and clear. It helped her regain a little of her equilibrium. Until she looked up and saw his gaze lingering on her lips. Their eyes briefly met, and the smile he gave her this time was pure male satisfaction. He'd drawn a response from her and he liked it. And dammit, so did she. In fact, if there wasn't a room full of kids right next to them…crap!

She walked to the door. Play time was over. Time to get back to the real world. Where she was on her own and knights in shining armor didn't appear out of nowhere to make promises they'd never keep.

"Hey, can we talk again? About the foundation? Maybe be a sounding board for finalizing things before I pitch it to my parents?" Elliot asked.

Say no, say no, say no. "Sure, sounds great."

Elliot beamed at her. He leaned in and planted a quick, sweet kiss on her cheek. "I'll see you later, Lena."

Her name on his lips sent a tremor through her, like he'd run his finger lightly up her spine. If they hadn't been in front of the day care, she would have turned around and plastered herself against him. Run her hands over every inch of his body. Discovered what other amazing things he could do with that mouth.

But they did have an audience, one of whom was the little boy she'd never in a million years want to disappoint or embarrass. So she shoved those tantalizing thoughts as far down as she could get them and stepped away from him. Maybe it would be better to avoid him for the rest of the week. The last thing she wanted was for Tyler to actually see an ill-advised public display of inappropriate lust. He'd just get attached and confused. Hell, so would she. Better if she just kept away, for all their sakes.

"Bye, Elliot," she said, her voice not quite as steady as it had been a moment before.

She turned the doorknob and left him smiling in the hallway.

Chapter Five

Elliot watched the clock, waiting while the minutes ticked by at an insanely slow pace. After Lena left him outside the day care center with a raging case of blue balls and a hard-on that hadn't gone away until long after he'd returned to his room, she'd proceeded to do her best to avoid him. He didn't know what the hell gave, because she was *obviously* into him, too. But he hadn't been able to get her alone for the rest of the day. And that morning he'd missed her by seconds at breakfast, only catching a glimpse of her beet red face as she and Tyler high-tailed it out of the dining room.

But she couldn't avoid him now. It had been declared mandatory for all wedding party members to attend the dance lessons that had come as part of the wedding package. His mother might not have been thrilled about her last daughter marrying someone like Oz, but throwing anything less than a spectacular wedding was beneath her. So, everyone involved in the wedding would learn how to hold their own on the dance floor whether they liked it or not.

Elliot had been less than excited. He knew how to dance. But now, it was a total godsend. Lena couldn't get out of it anymore than he could. Even better, the bridesmaids and groomsmen were expected to dance with the one they'd be walking down the aisle with. As the brother of the bride and the sister of the groom, Elliot and Lena were a matched pair. He'd be able to spend at least an hour with Lena in his arms, and there was nothing she could do about it unless she wanted to face the wrath of his mother. And *nobody* wanted to do that.

There was not a drop of guilt in him for using the lesson as an opportunity to get closer to Lena. He'd felt her reaction when they'd kissed. She was just as drawn to him as he to her. He knew Tyler made things…complicated. But not touching her again sent a streak of something remarkably like panic coursing through him. He didn't want to examine the strength of that emotion too closely. But he wasn't willing to let her go so easily.

The clock finally hit 10:45, and he jumped up and headed out the door. He tried not to rush, but he still ended up being the first person in the ballroom. The instructor greeted him politely and returned to setting up the music. Elliot shoved his hands into his pockets and rocked on the balls of his feet, needing some sort of outlet for the nervous energy running through him.

Oz and Cher showed up next, a few more of the wedding party filtering in behind them. Cher's eyes widened in surprise. She came over and gave him a quick hug.

"Didn't think you'd show up at all, let alone be the first

one here."

Elliot fought to keep his face neutral. "It's your wedding. I don't want to shame you on the dance floor." He winked at her.

She snorted. "Yeah, right. You could dance circles around everyone here."

"True. But Mom declared we all be here, so here I be. Maybe I can teach the instructors a thing or two."

"I don't doubt it," Cher said, laughing.

Lena walked in, holding Tyler's hand, and Elliot's blood raced. She looked around the room with a polite smile. And then she saw him and froze. She met his gaze, and Elliot's world narrowed down until he saw no one but her. They stood like two statues, just staring at each other. His heart beat in his ears, drowning out everything else.

"Elliot?"

He blinked, his eyes flicking to his sister and then back to Lena. Her cheeks flamed red, and she looked at the floor, then glanced around like she was making sure no one had seen them staring at each other.

"Elliot? Hello?" Cher said again.

Elliot turned to find Cher looking back and forth between him and Lena before turning a speculating look to her soon-to-be husband. Oz must have been watching them watch each other, too, though his look had a little less speculation and a lot more big brother protective instinct packed into the frown he aimed at Elliot.

Elliot cleared his throat and backed away. "Looks like my partner is here," he said, making his escape as quickly as possible.

He felt like he should be reassuring Oz that his intentions

toward Lena were honorable or something. Except one, he had no idea what his intentions were, long term at least, and two, if anything besides a kiss was going to happen between them, it was probably something he should discuss with Lena first. And she didn't seem to want to discuss what had happened between them at all, let alone let anything else happen. Something he sincerely hoped he could change her mind about.

He came to a stop right in front of her, watching with growing amusement as she tried to look everywhere but directly at him.

"Elliot!" Tyler said, beaming up at him.

"Hey there, little man. How's it going today?"

Tyler pouted. "I have to dance with a girl."

Elliot laughed and squatted down so he was on the same level as Tyler. "Ah, it's not that bad."

Tyler didn't look like he believed him. "Really?"

"Really. In fact, it can be a lot of fun. Especially if you are dancing with the *right* girl."

He glanced up at Lena, and she looked back at him, her forehead creasing. She didn't look angry. More puzzled. He knew the feeling.

Tyler mulled that statement over for a second. "I have to dance with Abby. I played with her at day care yesterday."

He pointed at the flower girl who was sitting on the floor with her elbows on her knees and her chin on her hands.

"She looks nice enough."

Tyler shrugged. "I guess."

"Did you have fun with her at day care?"

"Yeah," Tyler said. He frowned, like he expected Elliot to trick him somehow.

"Well, this isn't that much different from playing. You get to dance to some awesome music. You just have to do it standing next to her."

"Oh. Well, that doesn't sound too bad, I guess."

"Why don't you go over there and say hi? I bet she'll be happy to see another kid here. She'll be more fun to hang around with than all us boring adults."

"You aren't boring," he said, grinning up at Elliot. "Can we go play video games again in your room?"

"No," Lena said. "We talked about this, Tyler. We're supposed to do our dance lessons right now. We can do something fun later."

Tyler sighed. "Okay. Can Elliot do something fun with us?"

"I'd love to," Elliot cut in, before Lena could say no again.

"We'll see," she said.

"That means no," Tyler whispered to him.

Elliot ruffled his hair. "I'll see what I can do to change her mind. Go on over and get your dance partner. I think lessons are about to start."

Tyler let go of his mom's hand. "Okay."

He ran off without looking back, and Elliot stood up, his full attention on Lena now that Tyler was happily settled with his friend.

"Hello there," he said, his voice deep and low, not much louder than a whisper.

"Hi." She was still looking somewhere around the vicinity of his throat.

"I wasn't sure you were going to come. You've been avoiding me."

Her gaze finally met his. "No, I haven't."

He raised his eyebrows, amused.

She blushed. "Okay, maybe I have. I just... I wasn't sure... I mean after what happened..."

Elliot stepped a little closer, reaching out so he could run his hands down her arms. "You mean when I kissed you?"

She shivered, her skin erupting in goose bumps, though he knew she couldn't possibly be cold. The hotel was air-conditioned, but with so many open walls the steamy heat that lay just beyond the cool barriers of the indoors always trickled into the interior.

"Yes," she murmured, moving her gaze back to his throat.

He gently raised her chin so he could meet her eyes again. "Do you regret kissing me?"

She looked at him a moment before answering. "No," she said, that gorgeous blush staining her cheeks again.

Happiness streaked through Elliot so strongly he wanted to laugh with the sheer joy of it.

He leaned forward so he could whisper into her ear. "Do you have any idea how badly I want to taste that sweet mouth of yours again? Right now?" He kissed the soft skin beneath her ear, and she shivered again, leaning into him, turning her face so their cheeks brushed together.

She stepped back before their lips met and opened her mouth to say something, but before she could, Oz loomed up next to him. His stony gaze fixed on Elliot's hands touching his sister. Elliot dropped his hand from her cheek but dragged the other down her arm to take her hand in his.

"Everything okay?" Oz asked her.

"Yep, fine." Lena's voice was faint but steady. Her hand gripped his tighter.

Elliot nodded. "Everything's fine." He pulled on her hand, leading her onto the dance floor. "Looks like it's lesson time."

Oz looked like he wanted to say something, but Cher came over and wrapped her arms around his waist. Oz looked down at her and the frown immediately smoothed away, replaced by such a tender, loving smile that Elliot's heart almost hurt. Happiness for his sister filled him, and for the first time he wondered what it would be like to have someone staring up at him with such incredible love shining from her face. He'd avoided that scenario like the plague his whole life. Or maybe he'd thought he was avoiding it, but had never found someone who he wanted to look at him like that.

"They look happy, don't they?" Lena said.

Elliot's face softened. "Yes, they do."

"I was worried at first. They're so different. From two different worlds."

Elliot looked down at her, concerned at her tone. What was she getting at? "Yeah, I suppose."

She gazed up into his eyes. "They seem to be making it work."

"Yes, they are." A glimmer of hope and unease flickered through him again. Part of him wanted very much to see how things would play out between them. But the part that knew he had no business trying to be any sort of a father figure to a child made a small, hard knot twist in his gut.

Before either one could say anything else, the dance mistress clapped her hands and started barking instructions at them. She went from couple to couple, making sure everyone's hands were placed correctly. Elliot pulled Lena into his arms, one hand cradling hers, the other low on her back, but not so low that she'd find it inappropriate.

Truthfully, the temptation to run his hand down her back, following her lines over her hips so he could caress the amazing swell of her backside, was so strong he almost had to clench his hand to keep from doing it. But he didn't want to screw this up with her, and grabbing her ass like some kind of horny teenager would definitely not make the impression he was going for.

The instructor turned on the music, and the strains of a classical waltz filled the room. She started counting out the steps, and Elliot tightened his hold on Lena, leading her through the dance.

Childish laughter peeled out, and he looked over to see Tyler, his little hands holding Abby in an imitation of the grown-ups, leading her through the dance. They kept tripping over each other's toes and spinning around far too quickly. But they seemed to be having a great time.

Elliot laughed. "They're actually doing a pretty good job."

"Yeah, I'm kind of impressed."

He pulled her in a little closer. Her expression was wary, but she didn't protest.

"I've been thinking about you," he said.

"You have?"

He let his lips slowly stretch into a smile while he stared into her eyes. Then his face softened, changing his demeanor from sex stud to casual conversationalist.

"You know, that bug bite stuff worked great. I've been thinking about some marketing ideas. I bet you could make a fortune selling that stuff."

She blinked up at him, confused at the sudden change in conversation. "You've been thinking about the bite balm?"

"Yes. Why haven't you ever tried selling that? It works amazing."

She tried to pull out of his grip so she wasn't pressed so close to him, but he didn't let her.

"I'm enjoying dancing with you. Very much," he said, pushing his hips against hers so she could feel exactly how happy he was to be there. "And we are going to finish this conversation later on, I promise you that. But since I can't do what I really want to do to you right here on the dance floor, it might be better to stick to a safer subject."

Her breath audibly hitched in her throat, her eyes full of the same smoldering desire as his. Fuck. What he wouldn't give to be alone with her in his suite. But that was going to have to wait, so he needed to get them back onto safer ground.

He let his hand slide a little lower so it grazed her hip, loving the catch in her breath at his touch. But he did need to get them back into safer territory. For the moment.

"So, bug balm?"

She broke their gaze and nodded. "Right. Yeah. I have thought about selling it. Even looked into what that would entail. But I just couldn't see a way to produce enough of it that I'd actually turn a good profit."

"Well, that's what I've been thinking about. You could start off small, like selling at local fairs. And you could set up a website. It wouldn't have to be anything fancy, and there are lots of places where you can get cheap domain names and web design templates or software."

She nodded hesitantly. "I appreciate the ideas. It's

definitely something I'd like to do. Eventually. I've already done some of the base work to get things started. I purchased a domain name for it a couple years ago. I just haven't had time to really work on it," she said, her tone civil but defensive.

"That's great." He'd known it might be a bit of a tough sale since she seemed so unwavering in her desire to do everything on her own. But he was just as determined to do what he could to help. He'd just have to persuade her to accept his help. A pleasant prospect, since his favorite means of persuasion involved their lips and hopefully a few other body parts.

Elliot pushed on. "So you've already got a start on it. I was thinking, some of the ideas you came up with for getting the word out about the children's charity might also work as marketing ideas for your business. We have the same goal. Getting the word out to as many potential donors, or customers, as possible. We could revamp some of the foundation marketing to work for selling a product."

She thought for a minute, her brow crinkling. But Elliot hadn't missed the excitement that had shone from her eyes before the frown had taken over. She liked his ideas. A lot.

"That's not a bad idea, actually," she said, her voice softening a bit. "Thanks."

"You're welcome." He drew her closer for the final bars of the waltz.

He was mildly surprised that he was enjoying offering up ideas to help her out, even though he'd only brought up the conversation to avoid thinking about sex. Her response might not have been the rousing excitement-filled celebration that he'd hoped for, but she hadn't totally been able to hide her interest or her enthusiasm. That little spark in her eyes gave him a serious case of the warm fuzzies. And he liked it. And her reaction to his other more recreational ideas was everything he could have hoped for, so all in all, it was a pretty good dance lesson.

The song switched to one with a slightly faster tempo, and Elliot grasped her hand. "Let's kick this up a notch."

Before she could respond, he spun her out, then pulled her back in. She twirled around with a little "eep!" and ended up back against his chest, surprised and laughing.

"What are you doing?"

"Having some fun. Let's dance."

Lena laughed again, holding on tight while he spun her, twirled her, and wrapped his arms about her. By the time the song had ended, Lena was breathless in his arms.

"You're crazy, you know that?" she said.

He laughed. "Yeah, but it makes life a lot more fun."

"I'll bet."

The instructor, apparently deciding they knew what they were doing, left them alone to dance through the next few songs while she focused most of her attention on the bride and groom. Elliot had never had so much fun in his life. He'd been to every hot club in major cities across the world. Yet, somehow, swaying to cheesy music in a hotel ballroom was easily topping his best nights on the dance floor. Because of the woman he held in his arms. Because of the happiness shining from her face as they twirled across the floor. Happiness that hadn't been there a few moments before. Happiness she'd sorely needed and that he'd help create for her. Not that she hadn't been happy before.

She was delightful. Always. But this was different. This

wasn't tied up with Tyler or with their business ideas or family. It was just the two of them, enjoying each other. Hearing her laugh and seeing her eyes twinkling with happiness because of *him* sent a streak of joy through him so intense it was completely alien. For the first time, he felt really needed. Not for his wallet or his connections. But just for him, for who he was. *He'd* made her happy. And that made him…elated. He liked the feeling. Very much.

If any one of his buddies had said something even remotely resembling the cheese-fest tumbling around in his head, Elliot would have given him a good swift kick in the balls to bring him back to earth. But he couldn't help himself. The disappointment that filled him when their hour was over was almost laughable. He didn't want to let Lena go. He wanted to pull her closer and kiss those smiling lips. Taste every inch of her until she was gasping his name.

He looked down at her. The music was over, the instructor giving last minute instructions. But Lena's gaze was firmly fixed on him, her arm still around his waist. And unless he was very much mistaken, a perfect echo of what he was feeling was reflected in her eyes. She wanted him, too.

Her hand tightened on his waist, and for just a moment she snuggled into him. Then she stepped away, letting her arm slide along his back until she couldn't touch him anymore. He grabbed her hand before it dropped and pulled her back to him.

"Meet me in my room tonight," he said.

Her eyes flared wide, panic flashing through them. "What? No. Why? No. I can't."

She tried to pull away from him, but he wasn't letting her go that easily. Smooth. He'd been way too blunt. And after their little dance-a-thon, she probably thought he was only thinking one thing. Which, honestly, he was. But that wasn't really why he wanted her to come over. Well, not entirely.

He wouldn't push her to do anything she didn't want to do, but he really did want to spend more time with her. Hell, he'd be thrilled to sit on opposite sides of the room, as long as they could talk. Anything else they might do together, well, he was more than willing to take that as slow as she needed to.

"Just to talk," he assured her. "My parents are going on their yearly European vacation as soon as the wedding is over, so I want to pitch them my ideas for the foundation this week. I really could use your help getting everything organized."

She frowned but didn't say no, so he pressed on.

"I spoke with the concierge, and he said the hotel has a great media center. I can even get charts and stuff printed out so I can do a full-blown professional presentation. But I need to get it all worked out first. If I don't do it now, I'll have to wait until after Christmas, and I'd love to get this moving before that. Our annual fundraiser is in January, so I need everything in place by then. Come on. I promise I'll behave, if you want me to," he said playfully.

Lena gazed up at him, a myriad of emotions flashing across her face so fast he had no clue where she'd end up. Her forehead creased, and he was sure she was going to turn him down.

"I'll need to see if my cousin can watch Tyler for the night so I won't have to worry about him if we work late."

Elliot pulled her into him for a quick hug, afraid to let her see the sheer exhilaration that he knew must be shining from his face.

She pulled away and smiled at him. "I'll see you later then."

"Can't wait."

His body nearly vibrated with the excitement pulsing through him. He was happy about getting the foundation stuff in order. He'd never been so excited about a project in his life. Thanks to Lena. He'd paid lip service to the charity for years. And despite his desire to do more, he hadn't done much about it. Until now. Until he'd met her. She was the one who'd lit the fire under him. Finally, he had a chance to really do something amazing to help others and do something meaningful with his life.

But more importantly, he'd gotten Lena to agree to spend several hours alone with him.

Life was fucking awesome.

Chapter Six

Lena collapsed onto the couch and pulled out her phone. Tyler had had his lunch and was tucked up in bed fast asleep. He'd outgrown naps a few years ago, but it had been a long couple days already and when he'd curled up on the bed and passed out, Lena wasn't about to wake him up. A few quiet minutes to collect her thoughts was exactly what she needed.

She had a missed call from Iris, so she dialed her back. A little advice from her BFF would be good. She had no idea what the hell to do about Elliot.

Iris picked up on the second ring.

"Hey, Len, how are things in paradise?"

Lena sighed and Iris laughed. "That good, huh?"

"You know, I honestly don't know how to answer that."

"*Hmm*. Does this have anything to do with a certain handsome brother of the bride?"

"Maybe."

"Ha! Maybe, my ass. What's going on?"

"We kissed."

"What? Oh my God, girl, give me the details."

Lena covered her eyes with her hand and groaned. Iris laughed.

"Oh, come on. If it's good enough it's got you freaking out this bad, you've got to tell me."

"You first. How did things go with your cowboy?"

"Nash? Oh, that's going to be a long story. A really, really good story. But long. So quit stalling and spill it already, Len."

"We started out just talking. He was asking me questions about some of my business ideas, and he actually seemed interested. I mean, some of my ideas have been kind of out there…"

Iris laughed. "Yeah, I know."

Lena grimaced but realized Iris couldn't see her. "Yeah, yeah. Well, he didn't laugh at me. In fact, he even had ideas on how to get a few of them to possibly work. And he wanted my input on expanding the charity his family runs into a foundation. He really loved the idea I had, and we were walking around this gorgeous botanical garden, and he was so excited about these ideas, and he's just…"

"Hot?"

"Oh my God, you have no idea. And then he leaned in and kissed me, and it started out this sweet, slow kiss, but then…"

"Then? You can't stop there! Then what?"

Lena was glad her friend couldn't see her because she was pretty sure there was a goofy, blissed-out smile on her face. "I have never been kissed like that in my life. My knees went weak. I mean, honest-to-God weak. I even got light headed."

"Oh, that's the best. You've never had that happen before?"

"No."

"And?"

"I had to go pick up Tyler, but we ended up kissing again and oh my God. I'm not kidding. I was ready to rip his clothes off right there in the hallway. I totally forgot we were in public, Iris. I was sucking his face off right in front of the day care doors! What if Tyler had seen me?"

"Did he?"

"No, but what if he had?"

"He's getting older, Lena. Someday he's going to see you kissing someone. Unless you plan on staying single for the rest of your life."

Lena closed her eyes and leaned her head back onto the couch. "No. I'd like to meet someone someday. But meeting someone someday in the future is a lot different than seeing your mom making out with some guy in front of everyone else."

"I wouldn't worry about it. Does he like Elliot?"

"Yeah. He loves him."

"See, no problem then. Maybe your someday is now."

That thought sent a quiver through Lena that made her breath catch. There were a great many things about Elliot that Lena would love to explore further. But she had one very important reason to steer clear.

"He only loves him because Elliot is like a big kid himself," Lena said.

"Ah. Well, that could be a problem. But only if you want to make it one. Just because you made out with him once doesn't mean you have to start picking out china patterns. You're on vacation. With a gorgeous guy who is apparently the best kisser you've ever been with. Which probably means he'll be the best everything else you've ever been with, too. You think of that?"

Lena snorted. "Are you kidding? That's all I've *been* thinking about."

"Good. So, go do something about it."

"Like it's that easy."

"It *is* that easy, Len. You're both adults. Just be up front that you're not looking for anything serious and have yourself a little fun. You are beyond overdue."

Lena flung her arm over her eyes. Overdue was a huge understatement. At this point, all Elliot had to do was wink at her and she'd probably come on the spot. "Yeah, well that's my problem. He wants me to meet him in his room tonight."

"Yeah, girl! Just make sure you bring protection. You'd be amazed how many guys assume the girl is on the pill or something."

"Iris! Just because I'm going to his room does not mean we're going to have sex."

"Why the hell not?"

"Because…" She sat up and curled her legs under her, rubbing her hand over her eyes.

"Great answer. Why else would he invite you to his room at night?"

"He wants to talk more about the ideas I had for his foundation."

"Uh-huh, sure."

"No, really. I believe him. He wants to pitch the idea to

his parents, and they're leaving right after the wedding so he needs to do it before then. He asked me to help him get things pulled together."

"Yeah, sounds like a great excuse to get you alone in his hotel room, if you ask me. Even if it's legit, you're still alone in his hotel room. At night. In a room with a bed. Be prepared. Just in case."

Lena's mouth went dry. She could picture what might happen all too clearly, and her body was damn near screaming at her to let it. But wouldn't that be irresponsible?

Finally, she sighed. "Nothing's going to happen."

"Sure. Just like nothing was going to happen in that hallway, right?"

Lena's stomach performed a few acrobatics at the reminder. "I don't want to go in there with a purse full of condoms. That feels like I'm planning to...you know..."

"Have sex?"

Was she a total chicken if she flinched? "Yeah."

Iris laughed. "You can't even say the words, Lena. You're probably safe. But I'm firmly in the better-safe-than-sorry camp. It doesn't take much to go from sucking face in front of a room full of preschoolers to doing a whole lot more in private. Especially, if the guy affects you as much as he apparently does, and most especially, if you are tucked away in a room at night with him. Trust me on this one. Just...be prepared."

Lena laid her head back on the couch. "Okay, okay, point taken."

"Good. Like I said, you are well overdue for a hell of a lot more to happen. You just need to get out of your own way and seize the moment. For once in your life, go enjoy yourself."

The thought of Elliot touching her again sent a fine tremor down her body that was only partially about nerves. The man knew how to hit all her buttons. And she wanted nothing more than to have him hit them again. Repeatedly. Until she came, screaming his name.

She trembled as though his hands were already moving over her skin. "I'll try."

"My God, woman! Go get your vacay lay before you explode. Call me later. Gotta run!"

She laughed but Iris had already hung up. Lena shook her head and tossed her phone onto the couch beside her.

What the hell was she going to do about her little meeting with Elliot? And where could she get a hold of some condoms? Not that she'd need them.

But…just in case.

Chapter Seven

Elliot paced back and forth in front of the sofa, glancing up at the clock every few seconds. Lena said she'd be here at eight, and it was already fourteen minutes after. She might have changed her mind. Frankly, he was amazed she'd said yes in the first place. Not that he was planning anything other than business talk. Not really. Yes, they were going to be alone, in his room. But he had no intention of doing anything that she didn't want to do. And he really did need her help.

But if she thought he was just trying to get into her pants, he couldn't really blame her. He knew his reputation. And really, when a guy asked a girl to come to his hotel room after the sun went down, it usually meant only one thing. What if she'd thought that was all he was up to and she decided she didn't want him? Or what if something had happened? Maybe Tyler got sick or something? Should he call her and make sure everything was okay?

But if everything was okay, then it would look like he was calling to check up on her. She was only—he glanced at the clock—fifteen minutes late now. She might have forgotten his room number and left her phone in her room, so she had to go back to get it and didn't want to call the front desk because they might think something else was going on when really it was supposed to be a business meeting that, yeah, okay, would be awesome if it turned into something else. But he so wasn't going to push that on her at all. In fact, he was going to be the perfect gentleman, no matter what, so he could prove to her that he was interested in more than that amazing body of hers. That thick, blonde hair that fell to her shoulders in soft waves. Or the gorgeous, sparkling blue of her eyes that reminded him of a really frosty Gatorade, the dark blue ones. His favorite flavor. That slender neck that was so sensitive she broke out in goose bumps whenever he touched her there. Or the gentle curve of her waist that he wanted to stroke his hand down until he met the curve of her firm—

Knock, knock, knock.

The sound startled him out of his mental inventory, and he jumped for the door, pausing right before he opened it so he could catch his breath and put his cool back in place.

He opened the door, and Lena stood there. She seemed nervous, her eyes looking everywhere but directly into his. She bit her lip, one hand gripping a binder so tightly it was turning white. The other had a death hold on the strap of her fanny pack, which was slung over her shoulder like a purse.

He knew how she felt. Somehow she made him feel like he had when he'd been a fifteen-year-old kid, in love for the first time. With a girl whose name completely escaped him because the only one he could think about at that moment belonged to the woman in front of him.

"Lena," he said, happy that his voice sounded mostly normal, if somewhat deeper than usual. "I thought you'd changed your mind. Come in." He backed up so she could enter.

She hesitated for a second, and he thought she might actually turn around and run. But instead she took a deep breath like she was diving into the deep end of the pool, stuck her cute little chin in the air, and marched past him. Once she'd cleared the threshold and made it as far as the couch, she seemed to deflate a little, relaxing as she looked around the room.

"Sorry I'm late. I wanted to tuck Tyler in, and he insisted on more songs than usual. I think he was a little anxious about sleeping away from me tonight."

Elliot had been on his way over to her, but he froze at her words. "He's not sleeping in your room tonight? I knew your cousin was watching him, but I thought maybe she'd go to your room. I didn't mean for him to have to sleep somewhere else."

She put the large binder onto the coffee table and took a seat on the edge of the couch. "No. I wasn't sure how late we'd be at this, and I didn't want to wake everyone to pick him up."

"Will he be okay? I mean, if he's anxious... Will he do all right?" The last thing in the world Elliot wanted was for Tyler to be unhappy in any way. But he was a little surprised that he was worried enough that he was completely ready to send Lena on her way in order to keep Tyler happy. They could meet up another night if the kid needed his mother.

"Oh sure, he'll be fine," she reassured him. "It's sweet of you to worry about him."

Elliot shrugged. "He's a great kid. I have fun hanging with him. It's nice to be myself around someone," he said with a laugh. "He's not nearly as scary as I thought he'd be."

Lena laughed. "No, he's not. Don't worry. He loves my cousin, and she's got a little boy about his age. They played right up until it was bedtime, and they'll be at it again at the crack of dawn. There's always that moment, right when it's time to sleep, that you really want to be at home surrounded by all the things and people you love. You know?"

Elliot sat next to her, draping his arm over the back of the couch. Available for cuddling, if she chose, but safely out of range if she stayed where she was, perched on the edge.

"Definitely. I love to travel, don't get me wrong. But there's just something about crashing in your own bed surrounded by your own things. I never sleep very well at hotels."

"Me, either. Something in common," she said with a hint of teasing in her voice.

"I think we've got a lot more in common than that."

She looked up at him. His eyes riveted to her mouth, and flashbacks of their kiss in the hall ricocheted around in his brain. He gripped the back of the couch in an effort to keep his hand from sliding down her back or running through her hair that she'd left loose and free. When she moved, the light coconut scent of her blonde waves drifted to him, and he closed his eyes for a second, savoring it. He wondered if she always used coconut-scented shampoo or if being on the island made her feel tropical. She'd said there was coconut oil in her bite balm, so she probably used it for other things as well. He should ask her sometime.

He took a deep breath. If they were going to get any work done at all on his presentation, he was going to have to sit on the other side of the room. She was too much of a sexy little bundle of temptation. He was damn near ready to cry because he couldn't touch her right now.

She relaxed back, her shoulder fitting snuggly under his arm. Their bodies touched all the way down, her arm rested next to his side, and their thighs pressed together. She fit against him perfectly, like she was some long-lost puzzle piece that had been made just for him.

He moved his arm so it was draped around her shoulders more than the couch. He waited for her to tense up or move away. If anything, she snuggled closer. She'd either gotten over her nerves from the hallway, or she was totally plastered.

He wasn't quite sure what to do. She'd brought her binder, and he really did want to work on his presentation with her. But with her cuddled up to his side, the last thing in the world he wanted to do was move. Well, that wasn't true. He wanted to move all right. Move until he was over her, inside of her…

Elliot closed his eyes again and counted to five. Make that ten.

She patted his thigh, and electricity shot from where her hand rested on his bare skin straight to his dick. He held his breath and tried to slow the blood furiously pumping from his brain to the vicinity of his shorts.

"Should we get some work done?" she asked, giving his leg a little squeeze before pushing herself off the couch so she could settle on the floor by the coffee table.

"Sure," he said, thanking whichever patron saint who watched over horny men that his voice sounded calm and cool. Because he was so not calm.

Lena flipped her binder open. "Ready?"

"Very."

One eyebrow quirked up, and Elliot gave her a little half grin. That faint blush crept into her cheeks, but she didn't look away like she usually did. Instead, she bit her bottom lip and let her gaze wander from his face to rove over the rest of his body and back up again. The sight of those teeth lightly grazing the tender flesh of her lip destroyed what little progress he'd made in controlling his baser body parts.

"Good," she said.

That one word hit him like a sucker punch to the gut. He wasn't sure what game she was playing. But he liked it. A lot.

Before he could respond, she turned her attention back to the binder.

"Do you always have that binder with you when you travel?" he asked.

She blushed. "Always. You never know when a good idea will hit. I'd hate to have an amazing idea and then forget what it is before I can jot it down."

"Good point."

"Okay, so here are a few things I was thinking," she said.

She started going through some ideas she'd had about his foundation. He leaned forward, resting his arms on his knees, and tried to pay attention to what she was saying. He may have even managed a few coherent responses, but he couldn't vouch for that.

What he did know was that her light tan brought out the gorgeous blue of her eyes. The sundress she wore exposed strong, toned arms and gently sloping shoulders. The crossed straps showed enough of the curve of her back that he had to lace his fingers together to keep from reaching out to feel how soft that smooth skin actually was. Her legs were tucked beneath her, her bare feet peeking out from beneath the hem of the dress. When had she kicked off her shoes? Her toes curled under for a moment, like they knew he was staring at them.

He wished he could pull those feet out and run a finger along the soles, see if she was ticklish.

"Elliot?"

He looked up, startled, and met her amused gaze. She'd obviously had to say his name more than once. "Sorry. What did you say?"

She laughed. "I was asking what you thought of that last idea, but it looks like your mind is a million miles away."

He looked into her eyes and shook his head. "No. Not a million miles away. My mind has been firmly in this room since the second you walked through the door."

"*Hmm*, then what did I say?"

He leaned forward. "I didn't say I was paying attention to what you were saying. I said my mind was right here, the whole time. And it was. I was just thinking about *you*."

He wasn't sure what reaction he expected from her. Righteous indignation? Surprise? Intrigue? Embarrassment? There might have been a touch of all of those in her rosy cheeks as her gaze burned into his. But mostly, all he saw was a heat to match his own.

"Come here," he said, his voice deep with desire.

She didn't hesitate. She gathered her dress up in one hand so she could rise up onto her knees and close the distance between them. Her face was set in determined lines, her eyes blazing with intensity. She didn't drop her gaze until she was pressed against him. She glanced down for a moment, leaning in. He parted his legs so she could wedge herself between them, getting as close to him as possible. Since he was still sitting on the edge of the couch, their bodies were almost flush with each other.

Just watching her come toward him had made him rock hard and ready. She leaned in closer. The full length of him pressed into her belly, and he fought the urge to close his eyes and groan. If he touched her, he would have an extremely hard time leaving it at a few kisses. She set his blood on fire. His entire body nearly screamed at him to touch her, taste her, make her his. But if that wasn't what she wanted, he needed to nip this little game in the bud.

She rose higher, dragging her body up the full length of his.

"Lena," he said.

She stopped moving and looked at him. He ran his thumb over her lips, which parted to drag in a breath that was ragged with need.

"Are you sure?" he managed to ask.

She came in a little closer, rubbing her body down his. "I want you so badly I'm aching. I want you so deep inside me I'll remember you every time I move tomorrow. I want you to make me come so hard I see stars. I want you to make me scream your name so loudly the neighbors call security. I want you, Elliot." She punctuated her words with gentle bites along his neck. "Right. Now."

His mouth opened in a silent gasp. "Fuck," he groaned, capturing her face between his hands.

His restraint disintegrated. He wrapped his arms around her waist and lifted her off the floor as he leaned back onto the couch. She spilled across his lap, half lying on him, kissing him in earnest now. Yanking at her dress, she pulled it out of the way so she could straddle him. The moment her heated center settled over him, she gasped and threw her head back, rocking on him. He grasped her thighs and ground his hips against her.

She cried out, leaning forward to kiss him again. He was pretty sure his heart stopped for a few seconds before it resumed pounding. If she kept it up, he was going to lose it right now, like he was a newbie with no control.

He dragged his hands up from her hips to tangle in her hair, holding her to him. His lips molded to hers, their tongues thrusting together, mimicking what his body longed to do. She crawled farther up his body, settling more firmly over him. He grabbed her hips again, this time to keep her from moving, and pulled away from the kiss, his chest heaving to drag in a breath.

She looked down at him, her eyes narrowed in confusion. "What's wrong?" she asked.

"Nothing. I just want to make sure you're really up for this. Because I'm not sure how much longer I can hold out."

Her confusion evaporated, replaced by that look a woman gets when she knows the guy is putty in her hands. Well, not putty. Something longer and infinitely harder.

She rocked on him again, and his breath hissed through his clenched teeth. She leaned forward, her lips moving over his as she spoke. "I hope you can hold out at least long enough so I can get you out of these clothes."

He pulled back, his heart beating against his ribs hard enough to hurt. His whole being screamed at him to keep his damn mouth shut and accept what was being offered like a good little boy. But he wanted no mistakes here. Lena wasn't some one-night stand he could screw and walk away from. It wouldn't be a screw at all. The words "making love" floated through his head, and for the first time he actually meant it.

"Are you sure?"

She gazed down at him. "More sure than I've ever been."

She eased her hand between them and cupped him, wrapping her fingers around him through his shorts. He sucked in a breath and jerked beneath her, thrusting into her hand. She squeezed him harder, smiling against his lips.

"Oh, that's how you want to play, huh?" he said.

Her laugh turned into a squeal when he surged up, keeping her legs wrapped around his waist as he carried her.

"Where are we going?" she asked.

"The bed. I need a little room to work."

"Wait."

He froze.

"Do you have…in my pack…I have, you know…in case you don't have…"

He laughed. "No worries. I've got a box."

Her face fell for a second, and Elliot realized that she probably assumed he'd come to the hotel prepared to have a little fun with some random hookup.

"I made a little stop in the gift shop earlier."

"Was I that sure of a thing?" she asked, a slight frown creasing her brow.

He kissed her forehead. "Not even close. But a guy can be hopeful," he teased. "I wanted to be prepared. Just in case."

Before he could say anything else, she squirmed in his arms, reaching up to pull him down for another kiss. He didn't wait for her to say yes again.

Chapter Eight

They made it inside the bedroom, but not much farther. Lena's legs clenched around him and Elliot sucked in a ragged breath. He spun, pressing her against the wall. His mouth worked over hers, and she moaned into his mouth. He ground his hips against her. She whimpered, desperate for more. His teeth grazed a trail down her neck.

"Ah!" she gasped, tightening her legs around him so she could press herself closer.

He groaned and kissed her again, walking them backward until his legs hit the bed.

They tumbled back, and he rolled them over so he was pressing her into the mattress, his mouth and hands stroking her into a frenzy. Her blood raced, igniting every nerve ending in her body.

He sucked at her nipple through her dress, and she struggled for breath.

"Tell me what you want," he said, his hand massaging

her other breast, rolling the nipple between his fingers.

She flung her head back, her body twisting under the delicious torture his mouth and hands were inflicting.

"I want you," she said, arching up so she could capture his mouth. "Inside me," she whispered. He rocked against her again and she moaned. "Please. Now."

"*Hmm*, so impatient." He nipped at her neck. "I want you naked first." He sucked her earlobe into his mouth. "I want to see every inch of you trembling for me," he breathed into her ear.

She quivered, turning her neck to give him better access. "You're a little overdressed yourself," she said, hungry for the sight of him.

"Very true."

He knelt in front of her and dragged his shirt over his head. Her mouth went dry as she stared at all his muscled goodness. She sat up onto her knees so she could stroke the hard lines of his stomach. He popped the button on his shorts. In moments, those were gone, too, and she was left with no question whatsoever about how happy he was.

"Your turn," he said.

She grabbed the hem of her dress and pulled it over her head, leaving her kneeling in front of him. In nothing at all.

His eyes widened as he took her in, and she was glad she hadn't chickened out on going commando. The look on his face was worth every draft that had blown up her skirt.

"You are so beautiful," he said, his voice deep and raspy.

He leaned over her, pressing her back until she was flat beneath him. He lay to the side of her, his hands playing with her breasts while he kissed her. She pressed into him, trying to get as much flesh into his hand as possible. God, it had been so long since she'd been touched like this. She'd forgotten how amazing it felt.

He stopped long enough to take a sip from a glass of half-melted ice water on his nightstand. Before she could say anything, he was back, a wicked gleam in his eyes. He leaned over and sucked at her breast. She gasped at the sensation of the ice cube swirling around her nipple. The alternating sensation of the ice and the heat from his mouth had her clawing at the sheets beneath her, panting for more.

His mouth left her breast and trailed down her body. He stopped to get another cube from the glass and then settled himself near her thighs. His hands slid up her legs, pushing them farther apart. He trailed the ice around her folds, gripping her hips to keep them still when she squirmed beneath him. The ice circled her clitoris, once, twice, before he pushed it inside her. Her heated core melted it almost instantly, leaving her tingling and desperate for his touch. The heat of his tongue replaced the cold sensation of the ice, and her hips left the bed, aching to take more of him.

He licked her in long, sure strokes, holding her hips against him so she couldn't escape, tormenting her with every touch of his mouth.

Two could play at that game.

He was lying on his side, his head toward her feet while he feasted on her. Only fair that she do the same to him, since he'd left himself within reaching distance. All she had to do was lean forward.

He tensed and then groaned as she took him in her hand and guided him into her mouth. She sucked him in, wrapping her lips around him and taking him as deep as she could before dragging her mouth back over him, her tongue swirling around his sensitive head.

His breath hissed through his teeth, and he renewed his onslaught of her. She pressed closer to him and sucked him down harder, faster, until he thrust into her mouth with a moan.

"Fuck!"

He sat up, hauling her back beneath him and kissing her until she whimpered. The taste of her on his lips made her quiver beneath him while he drove her insane.

"Oh, God! Please," she begged.

He ran his hand down her side, following the line of her hip to the spot where she most wanted him. He slipped a finger inside her, rubbing against that bundle of nerves. She cried out and lifted her hips, trying to bring him deeper. He slid another finger inside.

"God, you're so wet."

He kissed her, his tongue and fingers stroking her in tandem until that warm pressure built to a raging storm deep inside her. His mouth left hers and moved back to her breast, sucking her nipple between his lips while his fingers increased their tempo. She bucked under him, no longer thinking of anything but that delicious ache that was almost more than she could stand.

His teeth lightly grazed the sensitive bud in his mouth and she shattered. She grasped his hand, keeping his fingers deep inside her while wave after wave of her orgasm crashed over her.

He rolled over and got a condom out of the box in the nightstand, then slipped it on while she lay back and watched. Her body still convulsed in little aftershocks, her pulse pounding in her ears.

He leaned over her, kissing his way back up her body. "I want to feel you around me when you come next time," he said.

"Yes," she whispered, lifting her hips to try and bring him closer.

The tip of him rubbed at her entrance and she gasped, the sensation almost overwhelming with her body still trembling from the first orgasm.

He sank inside her, one slow inch at a time, and she grabbed at his back, trying to keep her nails from digging into his skin.

"Oh, God!" she said.

He eased back, retreating until he was almost all the way out, then with one thrust, filled her completely. She rose to meet him, wrapping her legs around his hips. He dragged himself out and back in again, over and over, rubbing that sweet spot that made her quake beneath him with every thrust. The pressure began to build again, deep within her. She couldn't remember if she'd ever orgasmed twice in the same night, let alone mere minutes after the first one. Her body was still on fire from the last go around, making every stroke that much more intense.

"God, Lena," Elliot gasped above her, his rhythm beginning to falter.

She rocked against him, meeting every thrust of his hips. One more stroke and she tensed, her muscles spasming around him from within.

He shouted his own release, plunging into her as deep as he could, once more, before the tension relaxed from his body. He rolled to the side so he wouldn't crush her, but kept her in his arms.

He pulled her against him and placed a tender kiss on her lips. "That was…"

"Amazing. Oh my God, I think my heart is going to explode." She laughed, dragging in huge lungfuls of air. She laid her head on his chest, loving the sound of his heart beating furiously beneath her.

He wrapped a hand around the back of her head and pulled her in for a kiss. "We are going to have to do that again."

She wiggled against him, more than happy to oblige. "Yes, please."

Elliot laughed. "Just give me a few minutes to recover."

"*Hmm*, if you must," she said, kissing his chest.

"I must."

She sighed. "All right. I'll be patient."

She tried, anyway. Turned out, she wasn't so patient. But that was okay. He recovered pretty quickly, too.

Lena looked down at Elliot, resisting the urge to give him a kiss before she slipped away. She didn't want to wake him. But lying there, his body bare to the sunlight streaming in through the windows, made her want to run her hands all over him. Again. She shivered just remembering everything they'd done together. She tightened low in her body, and she wanted nothing more than to wake him up and do them all over again.

She needed to go get Tyler, though. He was an early riser, and she was sure he'd be looking for her. That realization was like a bucket of ice water being tossed in her face, washing all her fantasies away. The previous night had been incredible. Like nothing she'd ever experienced before or would probably experience again. Everything about it had been carved straight from her wildest fantasies. But that was all it could ever be. A fantasy.

Elliot came from a different world than her. Sure, Cher and Oz made it work somehow, but they were in the same headspace. Their backgrounds might have been different, but fundamentally, they wanted the same things out of life. The same could not be said by any stretch of the imagination about her and Elliot. He was sweet and kind and, oh God, the sex was mind-blowing. But she had a child to think about. And Elliot didn't need to think about anything in his day-to-day life but himself. He didn't have to be mature and responsible. He could be as carefree as he wanted. It wasn't fair of her to expect him to change that because of one night.

Every choice she made revolved around Tyler. There really wasn't room for anything else. She spent her days worrying about being able to pay for Tyler's little league uniform or school lunches, not whether or not she could fit one more club in before she passed out. She was a mature adult with responsibilities Elliot would never understand. It wasn't his fault. It was just the way it was. She wouldn't regret their time together. In fact, it would probably end up as one of her most cherished memories. Something to take out and play with whenever life got too real and she needed a good escape. But it wasn't reality.

Lena looked down at Elliot again, at the faint smile that still lingered on his lips. There was no need to wake him. The conversation going on in her head wasn't one she needed to have with him. She was a vacation fling, and she was okay with that. So she'd do what flings did and slink away before things got all real and awkward.

She slipped quietly out of bed, quickly got dressed, and gathered up her binder and pack. She didn't bother putting her shoes on. It was early enough there shouldn't be too many people about yet, and she was only going back to her own hotel room. She did finally decide to leave a little note on the table by Elliot's side of the bed. Despite the whole one-night stand aspect, she didn't want him to think she'd ditched him. Then she pulled the door open and stepped into the hall, making sure the door closed quietly behind her.

She'd only taken a few steps when the door to the next suite opened. And Elliot's parents stepped out. Lena's face flamed bright red, the blood flooding her cheeks so quickly it made her lightheaded.

Mrs. Debusshere froze, her eyes taking in Lena's rumpled appearance, her shoes in her hand. Elliot's room was the only other one near them. There could be no doubt where she'd come from. His father's gaze raked her up and down, and his face puckered in disapproval.

"Good morning, Mr. and Mrs. Debusshere."

Neither one said anything for a second. His mother finally blinked and said, "Good morning," in a tone so cold Lena wished she hadn't spoken at all.

She needed to get out of there. "Well, I guess I'll be seeing you later. If you'll excuse me…"

She high-tailed it for the elevator and hit the down button. The doors dinged almost immediately, and Lena nearly sobbed in relief. She stepped inside, punched her floor and the close button five or six times, not relaxing until the doors slid shut.

What a perfectly shitty end to a perfectly wonderful night.

Chapter Nine

Elliot's head pounded. He rolled over, his eyes squinting at the clock. Seven in the morning. *Ugh.* He dropped back down, burying his head into the pillows even while he reached out a hand to search for Lena.

The bed next to him was empty. He sat up, instantly wide awake.

"Lena?"

No answer. But there was a folded note on the table next to him. He flipped it open.

Went to pick up Tyler. Didn't want to wake you. <3 L.

He put the note down. He wasn't upset that she'd left. She had a son. Tyler, of course, took precedence, but he would have liked to have woken up with Lena still nestled beside him. Maybe next time Tyler could sleep over, too, so she wouldn't have to leave in the morning.

Bang, bang, bang.

It wasn't his head pounding; it was some inconsiderate

idiot banging on his door. He sighed and swung his legs out of bed, grabbed a pair of jeans from the floor, and yanked them on. Halfway to the door it occurred to him what he'd just thought. That he wanted both Lena and Tyler to stay. Like some sort of happy little family campout. Where had that thought come from? If Tyler was there, Elliot and Lena certainly wouldn't be able to do half, if any, of the deliciously amazing things they'd done the night before.

The realization that that didn't bother him stopped him cold in his tracks. He wanted a repeat of his night with Lena. Hell, if he had his way, he and Lena would never leave his bed again. But the thought of her spending the night with no kinky hijinks involved appealed to him just as much. He'd really love to sit on the couch with her and Tyler and watch a movie or play some games and then curl up and do nothing but cuddle and sleep.

He snorted. Where the hell had the real Elliot gone?

More knocking.

"Elliot?"

He groaned. His mother. Perfect. Just who every man wanted to see after a night of mind-blowing sex.

He looked through the peephole to see if she was alone. Even better. His father was with her. So instead of spending the morning exploring Lena's body in the sunlight, he got to deal with his parents. It was too fucking early. He needed coffee before he dealt with them. Not that that was going to be an option.

Elliot opened the door and plastered on a welcoming face. "Good morning, Mother. Dad. You guys are up early."

He opened the door wide enough for them to enter and stood to the side. They both stalked past him, his mother

looking around the room like she was expecting a cheer-
leading squad to be hiding behind the sofas. *Sheesh, one little
party gets out of hand, and she never forgets it.*

"To what do I owe the pleasure of seeing you both so
early?"

His mother grimaced at him. "Cut the crap, Elliot."

Elliot's eyebrows shot into his hairline. He'd never
heard his mother use that word in his entire life. She must
be seriously pissed about something.

"What have I done now?"

She set her purse on the coffee table with a little *thump*
and then focused the full weight of her ice cold gaze on him.

"You mean *who*. We saw her leave, Elliot."

He wasn't sure what to say to that, so he reverted to his
default setting. Dumb denial. "Who?"

"Don't give us that," his father said. "Lisa, Laura… Whatever her name is. Nathaniel's sister."

"He prefers to go by Oz. And his sister's name is Lena,"
Elliot said, trying to keep his tone controlled and respectful.
It wouldn't help his cause any to anger his parents. But it
was painfully obvious they wouldn't welcome a relationship
between them, and that seriously pissed him off.

"I'm hardly surprised to find some random woman in
your bed. There's always a steady stream of them coming
and going from your apartment," his mother said.

Normally he'd have made some smart-ass remark or
inappropriate joke. But she was referring to Lena, and he
didn't find it remotely funny.

"Lena is not some random woman."

"I thought you'd have more sense than to get mixed up
with that girl."

Elliot focused on breathing. Yelling at his mother would get him nowhere. "*That girl*? What's wrong with Lena? She's smart, beautiful, independent, and hard working. What could you possibly have against her?"

His father snorted. "She must be incredible in bed for you to be wrapped around her little finger already."

That's it. "Don't talk about her like that, Dad. She deserves some respect."

"Respect? We just caught her slinking out of our son's bedroom before the sun is barely up. You've known her what, three days? And she's already spending the night in your bed."

"That's none of your business."

"Oh, yes it is. You are my son. It is most certainly my business who you let screw up your life."

"Why do you think she's going to screw up my life? You don't even know her!"

"Neither do you! But I know enough to recognize a scheming little gold digger when I see one."

"Where is all this coming from? She's Oz's sister. You remember Oz? He's the one marrying your daughter in a couple days. You don't have a problem with him, so why would you have a problem with his sister?"

His father piped up again. "We might be financing this wedding, but that doesn't mean we entirely approve of who your sister has chosen to marry. But at least he's gainfully employed and has a clean background. Your sister has always been somewhat of a free spirit, so we've been able to downplay this enough that it hasn't totally destroyed our standing in the community. Every family has one child who doesn't toe the line. But you are my only son. You will carry on the family name. What you do, who you spend your time with, matters. It's time to grow up and start being a little wiser with your choices."

The slow fire burning its way through Elliot's gut spiked a few more degrees. If this kept up much longer, he wasn't going to be able to keep his fury from leaking out.

"If that's your only criteria for being trustworthy, then you shouldn't have any problem with Lena. She's very gainfully employed. She's the hardest working woman I know. She not only works her ass off, but she's an amazing mother, too."

His mother released a very unladylike snort. "She's a no-class nobody who got knocked up by some loser, and now she's looking for a nice rich daddy for her offspring."

Elliot's mouth dropped open. "That is one of the most hateful things I've ever heard you say. You have no right—"

"I have every right," his mother said, her face flushing with her anger. "You are *my* son. You've always been immature and spoiled, Elliot, but you've generally been careful enough to keep your conquests discreet and at least somewhat worthy of you. But this? *This* girl? What will it do to the family's reputation if this got out? What about your future? Your father and I have worked our whole lives to make sure you kids had the best of everything, always. I don't know why you and your sister are so determined to throw that all away. It's too late for her, but it's not for you. I will not allow you to destroy everything we've built for you.

"You might think it's just some island fling, but what if she thinks it's more? What if she ends up pregnant? Are you even taking precautions against that? I'm sure there's nothing that girl would like more than to have a child by you. Then she'd have a lifetime claim on you."

Elliot's hand clenched the back of the couch, stunned

and infuriated at his mother's accusations. "You actually think that she would try to get pregnant on purpose to trap me into some settlement?"

"We know her type, Son," his father said.

Elliot shook his head. "You don't know anything about her. I invited her over here last night so she could help me put together some ideas for our foundation."

His mother's lips puckered. "You've proved my point."

"What are you talking about?"

"You invited her over here to help you with a business matter, something she can't possibly know anything about, and somehow you ended up in bed. Did you actually do any work last night? Who made the first move?"

He couldn't answer that without playing right into his mother's hands. Yes, Lena had made the first move, sort of. But if she hadn't, he would have. She was not some sort of manipulative gold digger.

"As I thought." His mother gathered up her purse, and his father stood to follow her. "Your partying ways have gone on long enough, Elliot. Get rid of this girl. Get your head on straight. It's time to grow up and show some responsibility."

"I'm *trying* to do something meaningful with my life, our foundation, but you two have shot down every idea I've come up with."

His father gave him the look that made grown men piss their pants. For once, it had no effect on Elliot. There wasn't room for anything but the anger burning its way through his veins.

"Take something seriously for once in your life, and it will be easier for us to take *you* seriously."

It was all Elliot could do to keep from shouting right in

his dad's face. He refrained, barely. Somehow, screaming like a child that his daddy was being unfair didn't seem the best way to prove that he was a responsible adult.

His dad opened the door for his mother, but she wasn't quite finished with him. "It's time to grow up and get your life in order, Elliot. You can start by keeping your distance from that girl. She is not the kind of woman you need."

He shut the door on his parents, the urge to slam his fist into something so strong he finally turned and slugged the couch. There was just enough wood in the structure to make a satisfying crack and make his fist throb, though not nearly enough to purge the rage eating him up.

His parents had never believed in him. And yes, he could admit that he might not have given them much reason to in the past. But this foundation, it was important to him. And he was going to see it through, no matter what they thought. They'd put him in charge of the family charity. They didn't have anything to do with it other than writing a check once a year. And he was going to make something of it, whether they liked it or not.

As for Lena, well, they were wrong about her, too. No, he hadn't known her very long. And he didn't need to. No one had ever made him feel so alive. She was the smartest, kindest, most genuine person he'd ever met. She made him laugh. Made him give a shit about something for the first time in his life. Made him envision a better life for himself.

He shook his head at the walking cliché he'd become. Because damn if she didn't make him want to be a better man.

His parents were so wrong. Lena was exactly who he needed in his life. And he was going to do whatever it took to make sure she stayed there.

Chapter Ten

Lena managed to avoid Elliot until lunch. It was pure torture to do it, but she had to consider what was best for Tyler. She and Elliot would never work out, but since her body didn't seem to agree, avoidance was her only option. But there was no escaping him when the whole family was expected to meet. They had plans to eat together to get the schedule for the rest of the week ironed out. The dress rehearsal was the next day, and the following day, Cher and Oz would march down the aisle and make everything official. And then… It was back to real life.

Lena sighed and leaned back in her chair, sipping on her lemonade. Elliot had been seated near his parents, so while he'd spent the entire meal staring at her, they hadn't been able to talk. Tyler had gone off with the other kids for a little buffet the hotel put together for the children. They should be about done.

Elliot's parents finally dabbed their dainty mouths with

their fine linen napkins and excused themselves from the table. Once they were out of sight, it was like the whole table let out a sigh and everyone relaxed. Elliot stood, his eyes intent on her. Reprieve was over. He headed her way.

"Elliot!"

Tyler came barreling around the corner, and Elliot leaned over, visibly bracing himself for the hug that Tyler flung at him. He laughed and scooped the boy up, giving him a big squeeze while he jostled him around and then gently "dropped" him back to the ground.

"How's it going, big guy?"

"Great! They had chicken nuggets shaped like sharks and mac and cheese with noodles that looked like fishes. And this huge fountain that had chocolate in it that we could dunk krispy squares and marshmallows in!"

Elliot laughed but Lena groaned. Sweet heaven, the sugar rush her son had just described would take hours to burn off. She needed to find him someplace to run until he dropped.

"Can we go to your room and play video games again?" Tyler asked.

Elliot looked over at Lena, his eyebrows raised in question.

She glanced between them a couple times but finally shook her head. "I don't think so. It's a gorgeous day. You should be outside playing."

Tyler thought for a second and then jumped up and down, his eyes shining with excitement. "Can we go to the water park again?"

Flashbacks of the cool water lapping at her ankles sent a shiver down her spine. "I don't…"

"I'd be happy to take him, Lena. You could sit on a chaise and soak up some sun, and Tyler and I can play in the water."

Tyler beamed, his blue eyes, so like her own, shining like two bright little sapphires. She wanted to say yes, wanted to make him happy. But letting him get too attached to Elliot was a really bad idea. He'd already latched on too much for comfort. And in three days, they'd all go their separate ways. The last thing she wanted was for anyone to get hurt. It was too late in some ways. It would hurt her not to see Elliot again. It hurt her at that moment to see little creases of pain form near his eyes as he realized she didn't want him hanging out with her son. It hurt her to see her son's face fall in disappointment.

But it would pass. She and Elliot would go back to their lives and forget each other. Tyler would find something else to occupy his attention. But if she let him get attached to Elliot, that was a kind of hurt that wouldn't go away so easily. So she said the only thing she could say.

"Not today, Tyler. We're going to play with your cousins again."

Tyler's lower lip trembled, tears filling his eyes. "They are all going to the beach, but you won't let us go there, so we can't go play with them. We can't do anything fun."

He stomped away and plopped onto a bench near one of the koi ponds, his arms folded and his face turning bright red as he tried not to cry. Elliot looked down at her with a frown. He didn't seem angry exactly. More like concerned. But the last thing she wanted was to hash all her emotions out right then.

Before either of them could say anything, Oz came up to

her. "Elliot, can you watch Tyler for a few minutes? I want to talk to Lena."

Elliot glanced at her for permission, waiting for her nod before he went to join Tyler on the bench. Lena and Oz stood in silence, watching the two of them. Within a minute or two, Elliot had Tyler giving him a grudging smile. Another minute and they were both lying on their bellies, laughing while the fish swam to the surface to nibble on their fingers.

Oz nudged Lena with his shoulder. "What's going on with you?"

She glanced up in surprise. "Nothing. Why?"

Oz snorted. "You are wound so tight I feel like I could put you down in the middle of the room and watch you spin yourself out of control like one of those wind-up toys you get from fast food places. What's going on? Why don't you want Elliot playing with Tyler? He's a good guy."

"You sure about that? You were doing a pretty good job giving him the evil eye during the dance lesson yesterday."

Oz shrugged. "I'm your big brother. It's kind of a knee jerk reaction to want to beat off any guy who gets near my little sister." He grinned at her. "But Elliot... I know he doesn't have the greatest reputation. But deep down, he really is a decent guy. He might date a lot, but as far as I know he's always up-front in his relationships. He hasn't left a string of broken hearts all over New York City. I think I'd be okay if you two...you know."

Lena gasped, horrified. It was almost as bad as having the sex talk with her parents. "Oz!"

He shrugged again. "Just thought I'd put that out there," he said with a laugh. "Regardless of whether you two have anything going on, you don't need to worry about him with

Tyler. He'd never let anything happen to him."

"I know that. But you know how Tyler is. He gets so attached to men. It's like he's a new baby duck imprinting on the first male he sees."

Oz chuckled. "Yeah, he does get attached. But it's only for a few days, right?"

Lena tried to keep the heat from rushing to her face but failed. Utterly. Oz raised his eyebrows.

"Something I need to know?"

"No," she said as firmly as she could.

For once her brother paid attention and left it alone.

"Well, like I said, whatever is or isn't going on between the two of you, I don't see the harm in letting Tyler have a little fun. Look at them."

Lena glanced back at her son. He and Elliot had moved to one of the larger ponds and were flicking water at each other. Every time Elliot got sprayed, he'd do a goofy little dance, acting like he was melting. Tyler doubled over in laughter. He took a step back, a little too close to the water's edge, and Lena's stomach bottomed out. She opened her mouth to shout a warning, but before she could, Elliot was there. He scooped Tyler up in his arms and ran away from the pond in crazy circles. Tyler shrieked with laughter.

Once they were a safe distance away, Elliot put him down and started to run from him, making Tyler chase him. Elliot's arms and legs were pumping like he was running as fast as he could, but he was only moving barely fast enough to keep ahead of Tyler until he let himself get tagged.

"See," Oz said. "Tyler is in good hands with Elliot. I know he's like a big kid himself, but he's a good guy, Lenny. What would it hurt to let him hang out with Tyler? Or at least let him take Tyler to go play in the water, since that isn't something you can do."

"Oz," Cher called out.

Lena glanced over and waved at her soon-to-be sister-in-law.

"Gotta go," Oz said, pulling her in for a quick hug. "Think about it." He gestured at Elliot and Tyler. "They're having fun. Let them."

He left her to go join his fiancée, and Lena watched them with a growing ache in her heart. She was thrilled her brother had found someone he loved so much. But sometimes watching them caused twinges of jealousy. She wanted what they had. But it didn't really matter what she wanted. She needed to do what was best for Tyler.

She turned her attention back to her son, chewing her bottom lip while she watched him play with Elliot. They both looked like they were having a great time. And Oz was right; Elliot was amazing with Tyler. He'd gotten him away from the pond without yelling or scaring him or making a scene. She probably would have gone into full-on hysterics and scared the crap out of him. And never let him near the pond again.

But Elliot had taken care of the problem without causing a new one. Pretty slick.

Hearing Tyler's laughter ringing through the courtyard made Lena smile, but inside, the doubts and fears she tried to keep at bay started filling her again. Tyler looked so happy. He was running and playing and splashing through the water like a normal kid. Lena's frown deepened. When was the last time she'd seen Tyler so carefree?

He was a happy kid. Always smiling, always respectful,

always in a good mood. But as she watched him dart between bushes and rolling on the lawn, she realized that she didn't often see her son full-out playing. He was always careful, playing close to her, rarely straying too far.

What kind of mother was she that she didn't let her son just play? Or splash around in the water? Most kids liked doing that. And somehow, despite her crippling fears, Tyler still wanted to swim. She hadn't passed that fear along to him. Yet. But how long would that last? Heck, she wouldn't even let her son play at the beach when they were on a damn tropical island. She wanted to protect him, sure. But she didn't want to be one of those overprotective mothers who didn't let their kids out of their sight. And she wanted her son to have fun like all the other children were.

Well, then. Only one thing to do. She took a deep breath, ignoring the butterflies that had gone apeshit in her stomach, and went to get her son.

Chapter Eleven

Elliot had been looking for Lena for the last half hour, and the worry was beginning to get to him. When she'd come to get Tyler, all she'd said was that she had a surprise for him. But judging from the look on her face, it wasn't a good surprise. Or at least not one she was looking forward to. He'd thought she'd decided to try and take him swimming on her own, but they hadn't been at any of the pools that he'd seen. Cher and Oz hadn't seen them. He didn't bother to ask his parents.

He finally decided to go see if they'd ended up back in her room. When he got there, the door was open and a housekeeper was busy making the beds. She looked up when he came in.

"Excuse me, but did you happen to see the woman who is staying in this room?"

"Yes. She and her little boy went down to the beach."

Elliot's mouth almost dropped open. "The beach? Are

you sure?"

"Yes. I brought them some extra towels."

"Do you know which one they went to?"

The woman shrugged. "I suggested Kiddy Cove, since she wanted to take her boy swimming. No telling for sure if that's where she went."

"Thank you," Elliot said, turning on his heel and running for the elevator.

Lena face-to-face with the entire Caribbean ocean? No way was that ending well. What if she had another panic attack and fainted again? What if it happened when Tyler was out in the water? Something could happen to Tyler, and she might not be able to get to him. Dammit, she never should have gone without him.

Elliot hauled ass down to the beach as fast as he could go, his heart in his throat, anxiety crawling through him like some disease he couldn't shake. The resort owned several small beaches in addition to the huge stretch of sand that was the only barrier between the resort grounds and the ocean. Elliot didn't think Lena would choose one of the more crowded spots. With as nervous as the water made her, she probably wouldn't want a huge audience for her first foray.

Elliot took a few deeps breath, trying to calm his nerves. He wouldn't do her any good if he was half hysterical himself by the time he got to her. He tried Kiddy Cove first. It was a good spot for her to go. Probably full of kids, yes, but it would be more fun for Tyler to have other children to play with, and Lena had seemed determined to give Tyler a surprise he'd really love.

When he first reached the cove, he thought he might be

mistaken. He scanned the beach, his gaze traveling along the sand, picking through the family groups, one by one. No Lena, no Tyler. Then he heard Tyler's laughter ringing out, and he looked out toward the ocean.

The sight that met his eyes froze him in his tracks. "Holy shit."

Lena stood in the water, the ocean waves lapping at her kneecaps. Tyler was near her, but not close enough for her to touch. He was slightly farther out than her, the water reaching to his belly button. Lena's hand was stretched toward her son. Elliot couldn't hear what she said, but he could see her hand trembling even from where he was.

"Not good, not good, not good," he murmured, kicking off his shoes so he could sprint down to where they were.

Tyler caught sight of him before Lena did. Not surprising, since Lena's gaze was fixated on her son. Her face had gone so pale even her lips were nearly bloodless. She'd dropped her arm so that both hands were hanging at her sides, clenched into fists.

"Hey," he said, coming up behind her slowly.

She turned her head, keeping the rest of her body motionless. He slipped his arms around her waist from behind. She remained stiff for a second and then sank against him with a tremulous sigh. He pulled her to his chest, and she wrapped her arms around his and laid her head back against him.

"How did you know we were down here?" she asked, her voice thready and shaken.

"Housekeeping."

She managed a snort. "Figures."

Her body went rigid again. "Tyler," she called out. "Don't

go out any farther."

Elliot could tell that she was trying to sound normal, but he could hear the panic beneath her words.

"I'll get him," he said, letting go of her to get to Tyler.

"No."

Elliot stopped, frowning in his confusion.

"I mean, I want him within reach but… He's having so much fun…"

Elliot looked back at Tyler and had to smile. The kid had on a face mask that squished his cheeks out the bottom and a snorkel that flopped uselessly at the side of his face. He kept dunking his face into the crystal clear ocean waters, coming up seconds later only to dive back down.

Elliot turned back to Lena, pale and trembling but bravely standing with the ocean crashing against her shins, all so her son could have fun. He brushed a damp lock of hair from her cheek and kissed her forehead.

"No worries."

He headed toward Tyler again. When the boy came up for air again and saw Elliot coming, he excitedly splashed toward him, a large shell clutched in his hand. His legs were no match for the surf, and when the next wave rolled in it knocked Tyler's feet from under him. Elliot scooped him up before he went under completely and swung him into the air before letting him back down with a splash.

Tyler grabbed his hand, pointing to all the sandy treasures he'd been finding beneath the waves. The water was clear enough Elliot could see the bottom, and they spent several minutes digging their toes into the sand and seeing what they could unearth. Every few minutes, Tyler would run to Lena to show or tell her something. She did her best to show the proper enthusiasm, but her face was still too pale, her body still rigid. She was doing amazingly well. Tyler had no idea his mother was seconds from a panic attack.

Still, the fact that she'd ventured into the ocean at all was incredible. If she could stop thinking about the fact that she was in the water, she might actually enjoy herself. *Hmm*, that was a thought. The few times he'd seen her so distracted she wasn't paying attention to what was going on was when she was admiring some of his finer attributes. He wasn't totally naked, but his chest was on display for her viewing pleasure. Maybe he just needed to take her mind off the vast ocean lapping at her legs and make her think of more pleasant things.

Tyler ran closer to shore to lay his shells along the sand, and Lena turned to Elliot, gratitude shining from her eyes. He seized the moment and bent to fill his cupped hands with seawater. He splashed it over his face, standing up and running his hands through his hair while the water trickled down his chest. He shook his head a little, letting the water fly around him, like he was trying to cool down. Totally innocent, nothing to see.

Oh, but Lena was definitely watching. She still stood frozen in the waves, but her face was no longer deathly white. Her cheeks flushed pink, her eyes riveted to his. He gave her an encouraging nod, took a step backward, and held out his hand.

"Come here."

Her mouth dropped open, her eyes widening with fear.

"Come on, Mommy. It's fun in the water!" Tyler said, trotting back out to Elliot.

Her eyes darted back and forth between Tyler and Elliot.

She took a little step forward but froze again, her breath coming in short, terrified bursts when a small wave rolled in, splashing against her knees.

Perhaps a little more incentive? Elliot brushed his hands down his sides, like he was trying to get excess water off him, ending with his thumbs looped in the waistband of his shorts. He ran his fingers along the band to drop them a little lower, low enough that Lena could see the fine line of muscle cording at his hips. He worked hard for those damn muscles. Might as well put them to good use.

He left one hand on his hip and held the other one out to her. "Come on."

Lena took a deep breath and squared her shoulders. Elliot smiled at her, and she returned it with a hesitant one of her own. She walked out to him, her eyes glued to his. As soon as she was within reach, Elliot took her trembling hand and drew her to his chest. She wrapped her arms around him like he was her lifeline.

He brushed her hair from her face and cupped her cheek. "You are so brave," he murmured so only she could hear.

She tilted her face up to his. He leaned down with a tender brush of his lips. She sank into him, and he deepened the kiss, his mouth working over hers until she opened to him. His hands threaded through her hair, keeping her captive while he delved inside, kissing her until she moaned and trembled against him.

He'd never kissed a woman the way he was in that moment, and he'd kissed a lot of women in his life. With passion, with lust, even a few with a lot of like, and one or two with what he thought was love. But nothing had ever come close to what he felt now. It wasn't the heated kiss from their night together or even like the one in front of the day care center. There was no agenda behind it. Nothing but him wanting to show her how proud he was of her, how much she moved him, how much he was starting to care for her. It was more… real than anything he'd ever felt in his life.

He finally understood the moment Tom Cruise had jumped on the couch during the *Oprah* show. He understood every word to every sappy love song he'd ever heard. It was amazing. Exhilarating.

And scary as hell.

He pulled back enough to see her face. She smiled up at him, and the knot that had started forming in his stomach loosened a notch.

Tyler came running at them full tilt, his legs kicking through the water and spraying all over them. Lena shrieked and laughed, holding her hands out to ward off the splashes. Elliot grinned and grabbed Tyler under his arms, then swung him into the air to settle him onto his shoulders. Before he trotted them deeper into the surf, he wrapped his arm around Lena's waist and kissed her again.

"Come to my room tonight, you and Tyler. We can have dinner, watch a movie, and play video games or something. Just the three of us."

Tyler bounced on Elliot's shoulders. "Can we, Mommy? Please!"

Elliot held his breath, watching the emotions playing across her face. He'd already braced himself for when she said no. He shouldn't have put her on the spot like that. Especially in front of Tyler.

He'd decided to tell her not to worry about it when she

spoke.

"Sure. That sounds like fun."

"Yay!" Tyler yelled.

Elliot had to agree with Tyler.

"Thank you," he said, leaning down for another swift kiss before taking Tyler out to play in the waves.

Chapter Twelve

Lena tucked Tyler into Elliot's huge king-sized bed and closed the door most of the way behind her. She wanted to be able to hear him if he needed her, but since she and Elliot were going to work on his business proposal, she didn't want their voices to wake Tyler. She moved quietly back out to the living room area of Elliot's suite.

Elliot watched her coming toward him, and Lena tried not to be all self-conscious about it. But that was hard when his eyes followed every move she made.

"Is he asleep?"

She nodded. "Out cold. He played hard today. He fell asleep before I could get him into the tub. And he was so excited about it, too. He's never been in a tub that could double as a mini-pool before. I had him taking showers as soon as he was old enough to stand by himself."

Elliot laughed. "I don't know where he gets all that energy from. Don't worry about the tub. I'll drain it later."

"Thank you for today. For playing with him. And…for the beach, helping me in the water."

He took her hand, his thumb rubbing over her knuckles. "It was absolutely my pleasure. Thank you for tonight."

She tilted her head to the side, like she was trying to bring him into better focus. "You mean for invading your room, forcing you to watch kid movies, and play video games all night?"

He laughed again. "Yes. I'll deny this if you ever repeat it, but I think it was one of the best times I've ever had. It was a blast watching Tyler have fun. Maybe I'm not as bad with kids as I thought I was."

It was her turn to laugh. "You're not. You're great with him. But I know you're pulling my leg about tonight being one of your best times. I've heard stories about you and the epic parties you've gone to. No way did a night of Ninja Turtles and Mario Brothers top any of that."

Elliot sat back like he was shocked. "First of all, nothing is better than Ninja Turtles, just so we have that clear. They are turtles who are ninjas. 'Nough said. And Mario Brothers is a classic. Tyler's pretty good, too. Just don't tell anyone he beat my ass."

Lena laughed. "Ha! Yeah, that was a pretty great moment. Glad I got to see it."

"So am I. But I wasn't lying. I really did have a great time tonight."

"You sound surprised," she said, still amused.

He laughed a little. "I guess I am a little. I knew I'd have fun with you guys, but… I don't know…"

"No, I totally get it. When I first had Tyler, I thought I'd really miss the whole club scene. Going out and partying with my friends and not having to worry about anything else. And I still do sometimes. The cutting loose and doing whatever. I thought that staying home and hanging out with my kid would be boring or depressing or lonely. And it's not. Don't get me wrong, I love a little adult conversation at the end of the day. But getting to hang out with him and have fun... It might be a totally different kind of fun than I was used to, but it's a lot more satisfying somehow. Does that sound totally cheesy?"

Elliot shook his head. "No, I get it. I've been to hundreds of parties. And I couldn't tell you what happened at any of them. They are all the same. I'm not saying I didn't have a blast when I was there, because I did," he said with a wicked little grin. "But still, they all blur together after a while. But I don't think I'll forget the look on Tyler's face when he saw the Ninja Turtles for the first time come across the screen. Or how happy he was when he kicked my butt at Mario Brothers. That smile... That really gets you, doesn't it?"

Lena nodded, too choked up to answer for a second. He squeezed her hand and pulled her a little closer.

"Yeah," she said finally, "it does."

He drew her in for a kiss. Lena's heart thumped, sending her blood shooting through her veins so every inch of her tingled. He'd barely touched her, and she was finding it hard to breathe normally. She put her hand against his chest like she would stop him. He hesitated and she knew she should obey that first impulse, back away. But looking up into those sweet brown eyes of his, the smile playing on his lips, she couldn't resist.

She slid her hand up around his neck, and he bent down to meet her lips. He pulled her close, and she moaned and wrapped both arms around him, pressing as much of herself against him as she could. They slid onto the floor. He leaned her against the couch until her head tilted back to lie on the cushions. His mouth moved over her lips, his tongue dancing with hers until she was so lightheaded she couldn't have lifted her head if she wanted to.

Elliot pulled away first, shaking his head like he was having the same problem she was.

"I thought we were supposed to be working tonight," he said, though his amused tone indicated he was very happy with the little detour.

She didn't trust her head in an upright position, so she stayed back against the cushions and lifted a finger to point at him.

"Don't blame me. You started it."

He laughed, low and deep. "Very true. My bad."

Lena shook her head. "Uh-uh. You're good. Very, very good."

That surprised another laugh out of him. He leaned in again, but this time Lena did stop him.

"If you want to get any work at all done tonight, it might be better if we sit on opposite sides of the coffee table."

Elliot leaned into her until his lips hovered over hers. "Well then, I guess we'll just have to work really hard so we can get everything done fast."

Lena was pretty sure she knew the answer to her question, but she asked anyway. "Why?"

"So we can go back to playing."

She sucked in a breath and tried to close the distance between their mouths, but Elliot pulled away, winking at her as he went to his side of the table.

She pouted a little, but a shiver of anticipation ran through her. It was her rule, after all, so she couldn't be upset with him for following it. Or trying to get a little payback by teasing her. It did, however, motivate her to get the job done.

Forty-five minutes later, they had drawn up a solid plan for Elliot to present to his parents, complete with marketing and fundraising ideas and detailed to-do lists for getting everything in motion. They only thing they needed was the okay from the people who held the purse strings.

Elliot rubbed a hand down his face and looked at the papers spread around them. "Well, thanks to you, I think this foundation is going to be amazing."

"I'm happy to help, but it's not thanks to me. This," she said, gesturing at the table strewn with papers, "this is all you. I just pitched in an idea or two."

"You did more than that," he insisted. "And if we can get my parents to go for it, I think it will be a huge success."

"Then it's going to be a huge success. Because I have no doubt your parents will be eating out of your hands by the time you're done."

Those smiling eyes of his burned into hers. It was the kind of look that made her want to vault the table and jump him so she could do dirty, dirty things to him.

"A few days ago this seemed impossible. Thank you for your help."

He gave her that look again, and the parts of her she'd been trying to ignore for the better part of the night roared back to life.

He gathered up one of the sheets from her idea file— notes detailing the gift basket company she'd wanted to start once upon a time. "You know, this is a really good idea.

It's low overhead with the potential of making really good money. And there's a huge market for this kind of thing. Especially, if you've got somebody who can help spread the word among his well-connected contacts."

Lena tried to keep her face neutral while she processed all that. What he said was true. Not only true, but a good idea. And she knew her irritation was completely illogical. But…

"What are you thinking, Lena?"

She met his gaze, startled. "What? Nothing."

He leaned forward and traced the line of her frown. "That's not nothing. What did I say that you didn't like?"

She sighed. "It really is nothing. I'm being completely stupid. It's… Well, I've always tried to make it on my own. Nobody ever thought I'd amount to anything. I'm the ditz with all the weird ideas that never pan out." She looked down at the papers in front of her, knowing she was being unreasonable and ungrateful. "I just want to succeed on my own."

Elliot gave her that same exasperated look Lena had seen countless teachers give their students who couldn't get a concept through their heads. "Lena, no one succeeds on their own. Everyone needs a little help sometimes. And just because someone along the line pitches in an idea, or a re-ferral, or even some start-up money—"

Her mouth dropped open to argue but he held up a finger to keep her from protesting and continued speaking.

"That doesn't mean that you didn't do it on your own. The work is yours, the business is yours, hell, most of these ideas are yours," he said, gesturing to all the papers in front of them. "Trust me, it's coming from your brain. You'll be the one doing 99 percent of the work… The success *will* be yours."

She took a deep breath. He was right. He was totally right. She'd been trying to do it on her own for years and had never been able to get too far. Accepting help didn't mean she couldn't hack it. It meant she was smart enough to utilize a good asset when it came along.

Lena gave him the grateful smile he deserved. "You're right. And I'm grateful for your help. Do you really think I could make this one work?" she asked, picking up her gift basket file.

"Are you kidding? Gift baskets make amazing gifts. People are always buying them, and not only for holidays. They are great for employees and clients."

"True."

"I think it's something that could really take off. Especially if you let me help."

Excitement sparked through her. "You'd want to help with my business?"

"What I really want is for us to be partners with both companies. These ideas are more yours than mine, anyway. I just have a little extra background to help get them off the ground."

"So what are you saying?"

"I'm saying," he said, leaning toward her, "that I want us to partner up. We merge all these ideas we've been tossing around. You help me get this foundation off the ground. And I help you get your gift basket business going. We team up, work together, and make both these dreams come true."

Lena let out a long, slow breath.

"You think about it for a minute," he said, his tone

reassuring like he knew how badly he'd just freaked her out.

She leaned back against the couch and watched while he straightened up their paperwork, making piles to go back into their folders and a smaller stack to take to the media center in the morning to get some graphs printed out. It took Lena a minute to identify the feeling coursing through her, since it wasn't one that she felt often.

Contentment. Relaxing, happy, contentment.

Sitting here in the living room, quietly working on projects she was passionate about with a man she was *definitely* passionate about, with her son sleeping happily in the next room... It was the future she'd always dreamed of. That thought terrified her. Because for the first time, the dream felt like something that could become a reality. And not sometime in the distant future.

Their business plans were similar. She would love to be a part of his foundation, and he was interested in her ideas. They were enough alike that they could work together easily. Agreeing to merge their business ideas would tie them together in some ways even more firmly than a personal relationship. Personal relationships could end. Someone could always walk away. It wasn't so easy when it came to business.

But what if? What if she could have the whole package? She could have her own business, finally be successful enough to get her own place, support her own child without Oz's help. Spend her days with the amazing and incredibly gorgeous man in front of her, working on their dream businesses by day and spending their nights...well...doing whatever the hell they wanted to each other.

Her heart rate kicked up a notch. The day she'd spent with him was a great example of how the future with Elliot could be. And she liked it. A lot.

"Okay," she said, glad that her voice came out strong and sure. "Let's do it. Let's get your foundation built and maybe toss in some gift baskets while we're at it."

The smile that lit Elliot's face warmed her entire being. He stood and stepped around the coffee table, then dropped back to his knees beside her.

"We're a team?" he asked.

Lena nodded, her blood racing so furiously through her body she could hear her pulse in her ears.

He cupped her face in both hands and gently drew her up onto her knees. "You," he kissed one side of her mouth, "and me?" He kissed the other, and she trembled in his arms.

"Yes," she whispered, her eyes fluttering closed.

He gently pressed a kiss to her mouth and then sat back. Her eyes popped open in surprise to find him smiling down at her.

"Sealed with a kiss?" she asked.

He shook his head. "That was just the preliminaries. This is how you seal something with a kiss."

He pulled her to him, devouring her, his mouth moving over hers like he was trying to memorize every minute curve of her lips. His tongue darted between her lips, and he wrapped his arms around her tight enough to squeeze a gasp out of her.

"Sorry," he muttered.

"Don't be," she answered, wrapping her arms around his shoulders and holding on just as hard.

She climbed onto his lap, straddling his waist until the full, hard length of him nestled against her. The sensation, with all her nerves already on high alert, had her throwing her head back with a moan.

"*Shh*," Elliot said, quietly laughing.

Lena slapped her hand over her mouth, initially to keep her laugh from erupting, but when Elliot shifted, rocking against her again, she was glad of the barrier to keep another moan from escaping. She put a hand on his chest to keep him from doing it again.

"Hang on," she said, her breath ragged.

She climbed off Elliot and tiptoed toward the bedroom door. She peeked inside. Tyler was still sound asleep, curled up around one of the pillows.

The heat at her back let her know Elliot had come up behind her. He wrapped an arm around her waist and peered in over her head.

"Cute when they're asleep, aren't they?"

Lena leaned back against him so she could tilt her head up and see him.

"I mean, he's cute when he's awake, too," he added.

Lena decided to give him a break, though it was tempting to let him sweat that one out for a minute.

"Yeah, he's cute when he's awake, but when he's asleep…" She turned back to look at her son. "When he's asleep, I can still see the baby he used to be." She shook her head. "He's growing up so fast."

Elliot wrapped his other arm around her waist and drew her more firmly to him, resting his cheek on her hair. Standing there, looking at her sleeping son with Elliot's arms wrapped around her, made Lena's heart skip a few beats. But having him so close made her remember a few other things, too.

He wasn't quite as happy in certain areas as he'd been

a few moments before. But that was something she could fix. She quietly closed the door and then turned and took Elliot's hand. She tried to draw him back to the living room, but instead he led her into the bathroom.

"What are we doing in here?" she asked, her voice suspicious the closer they got to the tub.

"It's a shame to let all that water go to waste," Elliot said. Lena had never seen such a large tub in a hotel room before. It could easily fit several people.

She shook her head, panic starting to eat its way through her gut. "It'll be cold now."

Elliot dipped a hand in it. "Still lukewarm, which will feel good with how humid it is right now. Like taking a dip in the cool ocean."

"Elliot," she said, her voice trembling.

"You want to get over your fear of water, right?"

She stared at the full tub, her heart starting to pound so hard she was sure he'd hear it. But she nodded.

"If you can stand in the ocean, you can do this."

She shook her head at that. "That was just my legs getting wet. This is…everything, my whole body under the water."

"You can do this," he said, putting a hand under her chin to draw her attention back to him. "You're starting slow. A very small body of water. With something to distract you from the fact that you'll be in it."

"Distract me? Like what?"

He yanked off his shirt, and her mouth dropped open with a gasp. His shorts were next, giving her hardly any time to process all the deliciousness in front of her before he was suddenly very, very nude.

"Oh," she said faintly.

He climbed into the tub. "*Ooo*," he said with a little shiver. "It's a little colder than I thought."

She could tell. The moment he'd slid into the water, his nipples had pebbled. She licked her lips, wanting it to be his body she was tasting.

He pulled the plug and let some of the water drain while he started running the hot water again. "Better," he said, scooping up a handful of water and splashing it down his chest.

Lena's eyes stayed glued to the dripping wet god kneeling in the tub before her. She barely even noticed the water he was in. Then again, that was because she wasn't in it. Yet. She shivered, but she wasn't sure if it was from the thought of getting into the water or the thought of running her hands along every hard inch of Elliot. She glanced down and saw just how hard every inch of him was.

He held his hand out to her. "I won't let anything happen to you."

She stared at that hand and wanted to take it. She wanted to strip down and join him, rub her body over every bit of his wet nakedness. The water wasn't that deep. She knew nothing would happen to her, especially with Elliot there. But her fear wasn't logical. She was caught in a weird loop of terror and desire. One more glance at Elliot and she knew desire would win. But it wasn't going to be an easy battle.

"One step at a time, Len," he said. "Take off your shirt."

Her gaze shot to his, and he gave her that lazy smile that sent a fine tremor running through her body. If she could focus on him, maybe this wouldn't be so bad. She pulled her shirt off and dropped it to the floor.

"Skirt next."

She didn't hesitate, dropping her skirt so she stood before him in her white lace bra and panties. She'd worn something nice—just in case.

Elliot's breathing sped up. *He must like what he's seeing.*

"Bra," he demanded.

Lena let her own smile spread across her lips as she reached up to unclasp her bra. Elliot bit his bottom lip, and the sight was so unexpectedly sensual Lena gasped. She dropped her bra and lost her panties before he told her to do it, slowly sliding them off while Elliot's gaze raked over her. She let her hands trail back up her waist, then cupped her breasts, her head falling back with a sigh when her palms brushed across her tight nipples.

Elliot sucked his breath in with a hiss, and Lena looked back at him. His skin was flushed from the heat of the water, his chest heaving at the sight of her caressing her own breasts.

"Come here," he said, his voice deep and husky.

She took his hand, and a deep breath, and stepped into the tub. The water reached to her upper thighs. Suddenly, her trembling limbs had nothing to do with Elliot.

He didn't give her any time to think about it. The moment she stepped into the water, he grasped her around the waist, his lips skimming over the soft skin of her belly. His tongue dipped into her navel, and Lena's back bowed, pressing her body to his tantalizing mouth. His hands slipped down to her hips while his lips continued their journey south.

The warm water caressing her bare skin created an intoxicating sensation. Elliot's hands felt like silk stroking her beneath the surface. She still wasn't thrilled about there being quite so much water surrounding her, but she was definitely starting to see the merits. He ran his hands up the back of her legs, spreading them a little so he could reach what he wanted.

His tongue darted out, flicking the tight little bundle of pulsating nerves. Her knees buckled, coming to rest on his shoulders. He leaned back against the tub, helping her to settle over him. He licked along her outer folds, and a fine tremor ran through her body. Her hands threaded through his hair, and he redoubled his efforts. She gasped, her body rocking against him, trying to bring him deeper. His hands massaged her ass, using his grip to help move her over his mouth.

The warm pressure built inside her, her nails digging into his scalp. Her legs gave out, and she slid slowly into the water. He kept his arms around her, holding her close until she was settled against him. His mouth met hers, and she could taste herself on his lips. His hand fumbled for something along the edge of the tub.

Lena barely registered the sound of the condom packet ripping open. She kept their lips fused together. His hands reached between them while he rolled the condom on, and he guided himself to her opening. She straddled him more fully, he turned them so her back rested against the side of the tub, and plunged inside her in one stroke.

She wrapped her legs tighter about him, rising to meet each thrust. The water sloshed around them, but every time she'd start to notice it, Elliot would send some new sensation coursing through her body that shattered her concentration. His mouth moved over her breasts, his lips teasing her nipples, sucking and tugging, while he thrust in and out of her. His rhythm increased, bringing her closer and closer until she cried out, the pleasure exploding inside her until all she could do was hang on to him and tremble.

He came a moment later, his arms crushing her to him while he pulsed inside her. Lena leaned into him, her body limp and boneless, floating in the water. Elliot kept his arms around her, cuddling her.

"That wasn't so bad now, was it?" he asked.

Lena laughed. "No. That wasn't bad at all."

Truthfully, she still wasn't very comfortable floating in the water. But snuggled against Elliot's chest, his body anchoring her, it wasn't quite as terrifying as it had been a few minutes ago. And she did enjoy the heat of the water soaking into her body, the silky feel of Elliot's body behind her.

"See, you'll be ready for a full-blown swimming pool in no time."

Lena shook her head, rubbing her cheek across his chest. "That might be a little optimistic. This, though," she said, letting her fingers trail up his skin, "this I might be able to handle again."

"*Hmm.*" He tilted her face up so he could give her a long, lingering kiss. "Give me a few minutes and I'll see what I can do."

Lena smiled against his lips. "Deal."

Chapter Thirteen

Elliot sat across from his parents at the huge table in one of the hotel's conference rooms. He'd just delivered his presentation. Handed them a brief but detailed business plan in professional-looking folders. Gone through his entire idea from top to bottom. He'd done well. For the first time in his life, he cared about doing well. It was a good idea, and it deserved a shot. The fact that his parents actually seemed to be discussing it, instead of shooting him down at the get-go, stoked the little flame of hope in his chest. He really, truly believed they might say yes.

He should have known better.

He knew what his father was going to say the moment he stood up, before he even said a word.

"Look, Son, I'm happy to see you focusing on something…worthwhile for a change."

"But?" Elliot said, knowing there was a "but" coming.

"However…"

Elliot's excitement evaporated on a wave of disappointment so strong he thought he'd choke on it. He should have known. He *had* known. He'd just been too stupid. He concentrated on controlling his breathing, slowing the surge of anger that was fast overtaking his disillusionment. Losing his temper wouldn't help anything.

His father glowered at him. "However, we do not feel this is the direction the charity should go at this time. With the funds we raise, we help several charities—"

"Yes, but the problem is, we don't ever use the money for the same charities," Elliot cut in. "The charities we donate to can't count on us for funds every year. I'm not saying that the ones we choose aren't worthy of the money. But it's like we sprinkle little bits here and there on whatever happens to be popular each year. If we concentrate on one specific area, we'd be able to make a huge difference."

His mother chimed in. "The charities we donate to appreciate the money. Even if we wanted to take it in another direction, I'm not sure that I approve of the one you've chosen. There are those less fortunate and more in need of the help—"

"Are you saying foster kids don't need help?"

His father's scowl deepened. "Of course we aren't saying that. However, they do have funds for their care provided from the state. There are others who would benefit more."

"It's not nearly enough. Those kids—"

His father held up his hand. "For now, we'd prefer you to keep the focus on the way things are currently run. Everything is already in place and runs smoothly. All you need to do is keep persuading the donations out of our donors."

Elliot clasped his hands in front of him, his jaw clenching

with the aching desire to respond. Sure. His family was happy to have him on board. As long as he kept his mouth shut and did what they told him to do. No rocking the boat, no new ideas. Just sit behind the desk and flip the switch like the trained monkey he was. His family didn't really want him to be involved. There was just nowhere else to stick him.

But that wasn't enough for him anymore. Maybe it never had been; he'd just been too lazy to do anything about it. Until he'd met Lena. She'd made him come alive. Made his desire to do something worthwhile with his life increase to the point that he'd never be able to go back to how he'd lived before. She'd changed him. For the better. And he liked the new him. If his parents didn't… Well, maybe he didn't need them in his life.

He couldn't say a word of that to them, though. At least not at that moment. His sister was getting married the next day. He wouldn't spoil her day with his nonsense.

His mother stood and he followed suit, his manners automatically kicking in. A lady stood, therefore so would he. *Good monkey, treat for you.*

She walked by and gave him a kiss on the cheek. "You have a good heart, Elliot. You just need to make sure it doesn't get…misdirected."

He frowned. "What do you mean?"

She laughed a little. "Oh, come now. You've been running the charity for several years. You've never shown any sign of wanting to change things. Suddenly, you spend a few nights with that…girl… And you're full of ideas about foster children? It isn't difficult to see where *that* came from. I realize with her background, funding foster children might seem appealing, but that doesn't mean we need to let her disrupt something that has run perfectly well for years."

"First of all, I'm not sure why you think Lena's background would make her predisposed to helping foster children. Other than the fact that they are children who could use some help and she has a child. Oz and Lena never spent time in the foster care system. Their parents died when they were both adults. Not that it would matter to me if they had. Second, this is something I've wanted to do for several years. I was never organized enough to make a real go of it. Lena isn't disrupting anything. She's improving everything."

The disdainful disbelief on his parents' faces was almost more than Elliot could take.

"I find the timing of this a bit...odd," his mother said. "Up until now, your ideas had to do with making more money for the charity, taking what we've already established and making it better. Something we'd support if you came up with something substantial and executable. But now, that girl spends the night in your hotel room, and you suddenly want to revamp our charity into something unrecognizable. Benefitting one group of children instead of the many we currently help."

Elliot shook his head. "The charity doesn't help nearly as many as it could. The resources are spread too thin. Nothing is ever guaranteed. No one can really count on us. This plan," he said, jabbing a finger at the folder in front of him, "gives us a true purpose. Yes, it focuses on one group of children, but it's a group who can really benefit."

His parents' expressions didn't change at all. Nothing he said was making a dent. He shoved the folder away from him, exhaling in disgust. "You never had any intention of letting me do anything useful, did you?"

"Excuse me?" his mother said.

"You've wanted me more involved for years. I'm doing exactly what you wanted. I came up with a good, solid idea, and it's not just some whim I pulled out of thin air. It's researched and thought out and planned down to the last detail. There's no reason for you not to get behind this."

"There are plenty of reasons, Elliot. If you'd spent more than only the last few days paying attention to how things are really run, you'd understand that. It's encouraging that you finally want to become involved, but we are not going to restructure everything we've built because you slept with some girl and think you've had some sort of epiphany while on vacation."

"Lena has nothing to do with—"

"Enough, Son. I don't want this to turn into some sordid family feud. This isn't really the time or place for an in-depth discussion. We've given you our answer. Now, let's all move on and enjoy what we can of the rest of this week."

"And when we get back?"

"Like I said, your interest is a step in the right direction. But we aren't going to stake the future of the charity on you until we're sure this isn't another phase."

Elliot wanted to scream, but he kept silent. Nothing he said would help. They'd already made up their minds about him. He was a screw-up in their eyes. It didn't matter that he'd come to them as an equal, fully prepared and wanting to take the next step. You couldn't prove yourself to people who'd already made up their minds about you.

His father walked around the table and clapped a hand on his shoulder, giving it a slight squeeze before moving to open the door and wait for his mother. She kissed him on the cheek and followed his father out the door, taking with them any hope Elliot had of actually doing something meaningful in his life. His foundation wouldn't be developed. He'd just be a figurehead to charm money out of people—day in and day out.

And Lena… He'd screwed that up, too. His parents would never accept her any more than they were accepting him. He had nothing to offer her.

Perhaps it was for the best. No one trusted him with anything of any importance. He had no business getting mixed up with a woman like her, especially with a child involved. He couldn't even pull his own life together. He had no business messing up theirs, too.

He slumped into a chair, any confidence he'd had in his future had disappeared through the door along with his parents.

Lena paced down the hall from the conference room where Elliot had been ensconced with his parents for the last half hour. She had a good vantage point of the door. The second it opened, she ducked out of sight. She'd caught a glimpse of their faces, but it was impossible to tell how things had gone. They always looked like they'd been sucking on something sour. But they didn't look any more out of sorts than normal, so that might be a good sign.

She waited a few more minutes, but when Elliot didn't follow them out, she decided to go to him. She found him slumped in his chair at the conference table, staring off into space.

"Hey," she said quietly, not wanting to spook him.

He blinked and looked up at her.

"Hey."

She came around to his side of the table and leaned against it, close enough that he could reach out and touch her if he wanted. He didn't. He didn't say anything.

"So. How'd it go?"

Elliot gave a harsh laugh, rubbed his hands over his face, then shoved them through his hair. He stood up and started gathering his materials.

"They appreciate that I'm showing more interest in the charity, but they do not feel that foster kids are worthy of more help and think that I should keep my mouth shut and keep doing what they tell me."

Lena's jaw dropped. "They actually said that?"

Elliot let out a coarse sigh. "Not in those exact words, but their meaning was pretty clear."

"I'm so sorry," she said. She reached out to him, touching his arm, but he jerked away and continued to gather his things.

She tried to ignore his reaction and not be hurt by his rejection. His parents had really upset him. God knew they could be an ice-cold bitchfest of epic proportions. And a lot of men didn't want to be coddled when they were upset. It was hard not to take it personally, but she did her best to put that aside for the moment.

"I'm sure they didn't mean anything by it. Maybe it just wasn't a good time to bring it up. The wedding is tomorrow, so I'm sure they've got a lot on their minds with that. After they get back from their trip in a few months, they could be more open to—"

Elliot was already shaking his head. "No, they won't. They want me as a warm body on the scene, someone with the family name that can keep things going by my presence but who won't really contribute in any significant way. I'm the monkey at the switch. That's it. We were idiots to think this stupid idea would fly. Who were we kidding? There's no way my parents were going to go for this. It was ridiculous to even try."

Lena sucked in a breath. He'd loved the ideas they'd come up with, that *she'd* come up with. Her throat grew tight with tears she refused to let him see. This was all her fault. You'd think after years of coming up with one crappy idea after another she would have learned her lesson. It was bad enough she kept trying, but now she'd dragged Elliot into her vortex of failure. And sent him in to go up against his parents. What the hell had she been thinking? When he'd asked her for ideas, she should have gone with her gut and kept her damn mouth shut.

"I'm so sorry, Elliot."

"It's not your fault."

She wasn't so sure about that. "What are you going to do now?"

"What difference does it make?" he asked, his voice harsh. He had everything gathered up and headed for the door. He glanced back at her, frowning at the worry he must have seen on her face.

"Don't worry. I'll still fund your business. No reason for both of us to be failures," he ground out.

Lena gasped. He closed his eyes for a second and sighed.

"I didn't mean it like that," he said, his voice softer. "I just wanted to assure you that I will still help with your company, even if we won't be working together on the foundation."

She reached a hand out to him but dropped it before she touched him. He didn't seem to want her comfort. "Elliot, no matter what they said, the foundation is a good idea. Maybe we just need to—"

"No," he said, his tone leaving no room for argument. He pushed the door open. "The foundation idea is dead, Lena. Leave it alone."

He walked out and didn't turn back. She didn't blame him. She sank into a chair, struggling to shove all the pain rushing at her back in its little box where she could keep it at bay.

She'd done it again. Ruined something else. Why did she keep thinking she had what it took to make it in the business world? Hell, in any world. She'd never been able to make a success out of anything in her life. She should have known better. She still had the rehearsal and dinner to get through that night and the wedding the next day. Then she could go back home, back to her regular life. She could forget about Elliot, box up all her craft crap, and burn her idea binder. Elliot could keep his damn money. She'd rather work three jobs the rest of her life than take his pity money. Time to stop dreaming and wake up to reality.

Her dreams never became anything but nightmares.

Chapter Fourteen

Elliot sat to the side in the gorgeous courtyard where Oz and Cher would be married in less than twenty-four hours. The rest of the wedding party slowly filtered in, but Lena hadn't made an appearance yet. He jammed his fingers through his hair. He owed her an apology. The look on her face when he'd stormed out of the conference room that morning had been tormenting him for hours.

It hadn't been her fault his parents hadn't gone for their idea. They wouldn't have gone for anything he suggested, no matter what it was. He realized that now. But instead of making sure she'd known that, he'd snapped at her and stormed away.

He got up and paced near the staging area. The shame crawling through him was an unfamiliar and unwelcome sensation. And the thought that he might have hurt Lena in any way physically hurt. Like someone had his heart in a vice that they kept tightening. He wanted to make sure she was okay. Needed to make sure. It wouldn't change anything. But still… He had to know she was okay before they said good-bye forever. How he was going to get through the next day, he had no idea.

"Elliot!"

Tyler came bursting into the courtyard, Lena on his heels. She came to an abrupt halt when she saw him standing there, but Tyler barreled toward him at full steam. Elliot scooped the boy up before Tyler knocked him over. He swung him around and then put him back down.

Tyler grabbed his hand, chattering about his ring bearer duties. He even had the pillow to practice with. They walked back to where Lena waited with the other bridesmaids. Tyler kept up a steady stream of conversation that Elliot only half listened to. Tyler kept hold of his hand. And Elliot realized that the thing he and Lena had both been trying to avoid had already happened.

Tyler was getting way too attached to him. Not only that, Elliot was getting attached to Tyler. He was going to miss the kid when he went home. Like really miss him. That wasn't something he'd remotely expected. But…letting them go was for the best.

He came up to Lena and almost reached out for her but hesitated at the last second. The rest of the wedding party was gathered near the wedding planner, listening to directions for how the ceremony would run. He should probably pay attention to that, but he couldn't take his eyes off Lena.

"Hey," he said.

"Hey."

"You doing okay?"

She just stared at him, and the vice around his heart

tightened another notch.

"Where's my ring bearer?" the planner called out. She was getting everyone lined up and ready for their practice march up the aisle.

Lena patted Tyler on the head and sent him over.

"Lena?" Elliot asked softly.

She shook her head, not meeting his gaze. "I'm fine, Elliot. Why wouldn't I be?"

"Because I was an ass this morning."

Her gaze shot to his. "Not going to argue with you there."

He offered her his arm. She hesitated a second but couldn't really get out of taking it, since it was almost their turn to walk up the aisle.

"Look, Lena…"

"Don't, Elliot. You don't need to say anything. We both knew that this was just for fun. The wedding is tomorrow. The vacation is almost over. We'll go back to our own lives, and that will be that."

He frowned but couldn't argue. "I still meant what I said about helping with your business."

They started walking up the aisle, ignoring the wedding planner who was loudly counting out their steps.

Lena shook her head. "That's not necessary."

"Lena."

"No," she snapped, coming to a stop.

The couple behind them almost ran into them, and the wedding planner was waving them along.

Lena started walking again, forcing him to move with her.

"I don't want your help, Elliot. That's where all our problems started. The rest… That was fun," she murmured, her eyes darting around to make sure no one else was listening. "But the business stuff... I told you I was no good at that. I didn't want my bad luck to bleed all over you, too. I'm sorry I screwed that up for you. Let's leave well enough alone and just go our separate ways, like we planned."

It was almost the exact wording Elliot had thought of himself, but it hurt coming from Lena.

They reached the head of the aisle where Oz stood glowering at them. He'd obviously picked up that something was wrong. Elliot nodded at him, and Lena gave him a faint smile. He wanted to continue their conversation, but they had to split, her going to stand on the bride's side, him the groom's. They were far from done, though. As soon as the rehearsal was over, they were going to talk. He wasn't going to let her throw away what little he could offer her and Tyler.

He finally cornered her after dinner when the rest of the wedding party was on the dance floor. She'd excused herself to go to the ladies' room, and when she came out, he grabbed her hand and dragged her to a secluded corner hidden by a large potted palm.

"Elliot, what are you doing?"

"I want to know why you're turning down my help."

She sighed and tried to push past him, but he moved in front of her, slamming one hand against the wall to block her. She wasn't trapped, but she'd have to shove him out of the way to get past him.

She glared at him. "I need to check on Tyler."

Elliot shook his head. "I'm sure he'll be fine without your constant supervision for a few minutes. We need to talk."

Lena threw her hands up and nearly growled in frustration. "No, Elliot, he won't be fine. He's a child. One who is pretty good at wandering off and getting himself into trouble, if you hadn't noticed. See, this is exactly why…"

"Exactly why, what?" he asked, his gaze burning into hers.

She sighed. "It doesn't matter. There's nothing to talk about."

"Yes, there is. I want to know why you won't accept my help."

"God, Elliot! Why do you care? What difference does it make if I take your money or not?"

"It makes a huge difference to you! You and Tyler could use that money, and you know it."

"What is it to you? Some sort of pay off? You feel guilty for what happened between us, so you're trying to buy me off or something?"

Anger burned through Elliot, slow and hot. "That's a disgusting thing to accuse me of."

She folded her arms, her eyes blazing with her own anger. "Well, I can't figure out what else it is. Yeah, we had some amazing sex. That doesn't mean you owe me anything. Why complicate everything?"

Elliot stared at her. She was right. Why *was* this so important to him?

A child's laughter rang through the hall, and Elliot turned to see Tyler and Oz doing the chicken dance.

"I want to make sure you two are okay."

Lena's face softened. "We'll be fine, Elliot. We were fine before I met you. We'll be fine long after you're gone. You need to…let us go."

Elliot stared into her eyes. He wasn't sure what he was searching for. She hadn't said anything he hadn't already decided himself.

"Fine." He stepped back and nodded his head. "Fine."

She moved away from the corner, back toward the rest of their group. She turned slightly, talking to him over her shoulder. "You're a good man, Elliot. I don't regret what happened between us."

He nodded again and watched her walk away, taking with her everything that had made him truly happy.

Chapter Fifteen

Tyler slept peacefully snuggled in their bed while Lena sat on the couch in the little sitting area of their hotel room, a little wine bottle from the mini-fridge in one hand and her empty idea binder in the other. The papers filled with her ideas were spread before her on the coffee table like the world's worst montage. Here is your crappy life, in 3-D. She'd kept every idea she'd ever had from grade school on up on those pages. Dozens upon dozens of them. Not one of them worth a damn.

"What a waste," she murmured.

She took another sip of wine, wishing the mini-bottle was three times the size. There probably a good two glasses worth of wine inside. Enough to take the edge off the grief and overwhelming disappointment raging through her but not nearly enough to erase the last twenty-four hours from her mind. And she really, really wanted it erased.

She hadn't seen Elliot since their little talk at the

rehearsal dinner. He'd disappeared from the festivities. Which had probably been a blessing. If she hadn't walked away from him when she did, she would have either cried or thrown herself into his arms and begged him to stay with her. Both mortifying choices that she was happy she'd avoided.

She'd meant what she'd said. They were better off going their separate ways. She'd done enough damage to his life, and had he spent any more time in hers, she might not have been able to walk away at all. And then where would she have been? Sitting alone, nursing a broken heart.

She looked down at the wine bottle in her hand. *Oh.* She snorted. Well, it would have been much worse, for sure.

A quiet knock sounded at her door, and Lena's heart pounded in her chest, hope and dread coursing through her at the slim chance that it was Elliot. She stood up, suddenly wishing she was wearing something more than her favorite oversized T-shirt. She didn't have anything on under it, but it came down to mid-thigh, so she wouldn't be flashing her undies. Her hair was in a messy bun on top of her head, but she could run a brush through it…

Knock, knock, knock.

"Lenny, it's me. Open up."

Lena's shoulders slumped. Oz. She went to the door and opened it, no longer caring what she looked like. Her brother had seen her much worse.

She opened the door for him, then turned around and slunk back to the couch, leaving him to follow her in.

His eyebrows rose at the empty mini-wine bottle, papers strewn everywhere, and her general state of disarray.

"That bad, huh?"

She snorted, a sound that almost ended on a sob, but she

sucked it back in time. Tempting though it was, she wasn't going to sit and cry over a four-day non-relationship. She wasn't even sure that was exactly the problem. Yes, she was upset at how things were going, or not, with Elliot. But there were other reasons things were going badly—the same damn issues that had been a problem for her since day one. Bad ideas. Bad implementation. Bad everything.

She was tired of not being able to do anything right. She couldn't make a business successful to save her life. She couldn't support her son on her own. Hell, she couldn't even have a vacation fling without screwing it up and having everything get all dramatic and complicated.

"Len," Oz said, sitting beside her on the couch. "What's up?"

She groaned and put her head on his shoulder. "Same shit, different smell."

He chuckled a little and pulled away from her so he could see her face. "You might have to elaborate on that a little for me."

Lena grabbed a tissue from the side table and dabbed at the tears that were escaping, despite her best efforts.

"I'm so sick of taking one step forward just to fall ten steps back. It's like every time I think I've finally found a great idea that might actually work out, some ridiculous issue comes up, and it doesn't pan out. I've been trying for six years to make something out of my life. But I'm not qualified for anything. I can't do anything. Sure, I've got a million ideas, but they are all crap, and even if they weren't, I have no way of making any of them fly.

"So instead of being a good mom and providing a better life for my son, I have to mooch off you like some deadbeat.

I mean, what kind of a mom am I? If it weren't for you, I wouldn't even have a home for my son to live in. I hope you don't take that wrong," she hurried to add. "I'll never be able to repay you for everything you've done for us or express how grateful I am that you are such an amazing brother. You've always taken care of us. But... I'm his mom. I should be able to take care of him. But everything I try seems to crumble around me. Nothing works out."

Oz reached over and squeezed her shoulder and she sniffed, wiping at her nose. "I guess I'm just tired of getting so close and having nothing but a big pile of failures to show for it. You work so hard for us, and I don't do anything to help. You shouldn't have to shoulder it all. It should be my responsibility. So every time I might be able to help make life a little easier, and it doesn't work out... It hurts a million times more. Especially now that you are getting married. You should be bringing Cher home to your own house. Not the house where your sister and her kid live."

Oz wrapped his arm around her and pulled her in for a hug. She snuggled against his chest, feeling for a moment like she had when they were younger and he had comforted her after she'd gotten into trouble or been dumped by some loser. He'd always been there for her. Sure, he'd tortured her a little. What big brother didn't? But for the most part, he'd always been there, doing whatever he could to make her life better.

"First of all," Oz said, pulling away again, "take a look at your son over there."

Lena sniffed again and looked at the small lump burrowed against the pillows.

"No matter what else you do in this life, you will never be a failure. You brought that amazing little boy into the world and have been the best mother any kid could ask for."

Lena started shaking her head, but Oz put his hand on top of it to stop her.

"Yes. We agreed when he was born that you'd stay home to take care of him until he was in school fulltime. It has been a privilege to me that you've allowed me to help raise him. As for you guys still living with me and Cher after we're married, it's a non-issue. We've all been living together for the last year, and we are very happy to keep that arrangement. So stop worrying about that."

"We can't all live together forever, Oz."

"Why not?"

Lena smiled at her brother, though she couldn't see him well through the tears swimming in her eyes. "Someday you guys will have kids of your own."

The joy that lit Oz's eyes went a long way to cheering Lena. More than anyone she knew, Oz deserved to be happy. She was so glad he'd found Cher.

"When someday comes, we'll decide what to do then. For now, everyone is happy with the way things are."

Lena started to protest, but he ignored her, leaning over to pick through her pile of ideas.

"Oh my God, I forgot about this one," he said, laughing. He picked up a page that had one of those knotted friendship bracelets stapled to it, his grin stretching from ear to ear. "You wrangled every kid in the neighborhood into making these for you so you could sell them to the moms."

"Yeah. The parents weren't real happy with me after a while."

"Us kids were. You covered our ice cream truck treats for a month."

Lena grinned. "That was the first one that ever made money."

"Yeah. And you were eight. You've got to stop being so hard on yourself. Not every idea is going to pan out, but someday, one of these is going to take off."

She sighed. "I wish I believed that."

Oz held up another sheet, the one with the recipe for her lip and bug bite balms. "What about this one? This stuff is great, all of them. Cher refuses to use anything else now. Which reminds me, I was supposed to ask if you had any bite balm on you. She's got a few on her legs, but her tin is empty."

"In my bag," she said, gesturing to where it sat by the end of the couch.

He dug around until he found it. "Thanks. So, why didn't you go after that one? It's a damn good idea."

She shrugged. "I don't know that I could sell enough to make a profit after buying the materials, the business license, and insurance."

"So why don't you do a little research and find out? Maybe all you need is a good investor. Or you could do one of those campaigns online that everyone is donating to nowadays. A lot of people get the funding they need for their start-ups that way."

"Because I think I should stop wasting my time on ideas that will probably never pan out and get a job that will actually support my son. None of these ideas ever really work. Or haven't you noticed?"

Oz stared at her long enough that she started squirming. "What's going on, Len? This isn't only about your business ideas."

She tried to keep any incriminating expression from showing. "Nothing is going on."

His forehead creased while he studied her. "It has something to do with Elliot, doesn't it?"

Startled, Lena's gaze shot to his. "What do you mean?"

"You tell me. I know you guys have been spending a lot of time together. And I know he had a meeting with his parents this morning, and he hasn't quite been himself since. So, what happened?"

She sighed and leaned her head back against the couch. "We've been working on a plan to convert their family charity into a foundation that actually *does* good things for people. Elliot asked me for ideas."

"And did you have any?"

Her lips puckered up in a self-deprecating smirk. "Always. We came up with a foundation he wanted to call KidsCase."

Oz's eyes grew wider the more Lena told him about the foundation idea. "So, the two of you cooked this up and took it to his parents."

"He presented it to them. They don't seem to like me much."

Oz snorted. "They don't like anyone outside their own circle much. I'm assuming it didn't go well."

She bit her lip. "They're happy he's showing an interest. They just don't want him changing things."

Oz squinted, looking at her thoughtfully. "How much of all this was your idea?"

She shrugged again. "About half probably. But I couldn't have done it without Elliot." She fought to keep her voice steady, though her throat was thick with tears again. "We really were a pretty great team."

Her brother stared at her. "You care about him, don't you?"

Lena's mouth dropped open, her eyes wide. It was a simple question. So why was her pulse pounding in her ears? She hadn't even admitted to herself how much she cared about Elliot. How much she wished they could be together for real. Her few days with him had meant more to her than any other relationship she'd ever been in. And despite her misgivings over Elliot's complete lack of parenting skills, he was good with Tyler. The parenting stuff could be learned. It was that special connection that couldn't be forced. And Elliot had that with Tyler already. She would love to see if they could make it work between them. But that wasn't going to happen. So she'd tried not to even think about it. Tried and failed.

Oz nudged her shoulder. "I've seen you guys together, Len. I've been watching Elliot with Tyler. Watching the three of you together. It's not something I would've predicted," he said with a laugh. "But you guys work."

Her eyes filled with tears again. "No, we don't."

Oz gave her that I'm-the-big-brother-so-I-know-better smile. "Yeah. You do. The three of you together..." He beamed at her. "It *works*."

Lena didn't know what to say. She was afraid to agree, afraid to voice how much she wanted what he was saying to be true. She sucked in a deep breath. "Tyler seems to really like him, doesn't he? I mean, he likes most guys. But... It's different with Elliot, I think. More natural. Even though Elliot has no clue what he's doing," she said with a quiet laugh.

"Neither did I when you two first moved in. I learned."

Her heart melted a bit. "Yes, you did." She looked down

at her hands, twisting the wine bottle around. "I didn't think Elliot would be good for Tyler, or for me. But… He's kind of surprising, isn't he?"

Oz smiled. "Like I said, you three work. I don't know what happened this morning, if it had something to do with his parents or what. But whatever's going on… Isn't something that works worth fighting for?"

She looked down at her clasped hands. Did she want to fight for Elliot? Was Oz right? Did Elliot care about her, too? About them? If he did… She looked up at her brother, a smile spreading slowly across her lips. "Yeah. Yeah, it is."

"Good." He drew her into a bone-crushing hug. Then he gave her a quick kiss on her forehead and stood up. "I better get going. I'm getting married tomorrow."

Lena laughed. "Go get your beauty sleep. Cher'll kill you if you look horrible for the pictures."

Oz winked at her. "Not possible for this to look horrible," he said, waving his hands at his body like he was the main prize on some game show. Then he sobered a little. "It took me a while, you know. But looks like I'm finally going to see something that works all the way through to the end myself."

Lena gave him another hug.

"Love you, Ozzie."

"Love you, too, Lenny." He opened the door. "See you at the wedding," he called over his shoulder.

Lena wrapped her arms around herself. So… Oz thought she and Elliot worked, huh? Looks like she had a lot of thinking to do. Because she was having a hard time talking herself out of believing it, too.

Chapter Sixteen

Elliot took another sip of his drink, some ridiculous tropical thing that he'd only ordered because it came in a coconut. And coconuts reminded him of Lena. He hadn't realized that was why he'd ordered it until he'd taken a drink and the coconut scent had wafted over him. The smell made his heart clench with the memory of the scent in Lena's hair. On her lips. Her skin.

He took another sip, letting it linger in his mouth so he could savor it.

He didn't notice anyone had sat next to him until she spoke. "If you are too drunk to walk down the aisle tomorrow, I'm going to be pissed."

Elliot saluted his sister with the coconut and took another drink. "I promise I will be able to walk down the aisle."

"Not if you keep drinking that thing, you won't."

"I didn't say I'd be able to walk well."

Cher shook her head, but she couldn't help but smile.

"Give me that." She took it from him, sniffed it, and took a sip.

"*Heh.* Not bad. A little fruitier than I thought you liked."

He shrugged. "I was in the mood for coconut."

Cher looked amused. "I bet you were."

Elliot's eyes narrowed, trying to figure out what she meant. The words might be innocent, but there was a smug undertone to them. Then again, he might not want to know what she meant. Cher had always had a certain intuition when it came to him. Maybe it was a twin thing. Whatever it was, she always seemed to know what was wrong with him before he did. Although in this case he was pretty well aware what was wrong, and he didn't feel like delving into it too deeply.

He'd really screwed things up with Lena. He'd let his anger and disappointment over his parents' rejection of their plan get the better of him. He let his doubts about himself and his future cloud his decisions over Lena and any possible future with her. And shutting her out after everything she'd done to help him, and after everything they'd done together, was inexcusable.

And then trying to make up for it by trying to force her to accept his help with her own business. Yes, he could admit it had partially been a way to keep her in his life. But that had never been the plan to begin with. They were just supposed to have a little fun. So why did he feel like absolute shit?

The problem was… He didn't know what to do about her. He knew how he felt when he was with her. And with Tyler. But how did that translate into a relationship? How would it even work with them? They lived a thousand miles apart. And thinking of how his parents would react made his skin crawl.

He sighed and took his drink back from his sister, draining the last of it and signaling the bartender to bring him another one. He had no idea how to have a healthy, long-lasting relationship. Hell, until he'd met Lena it had never occurred to him that he'd want one. Let alone one that included a kid. Being with Lena meant jumping right in, with both feet.

"Come on. What's up, Smelliot?" Cherice asked, using her childhood nickname for him.

The bartender brought him a new coconut, and he twirled it in his hands. "Are you happy, Cher?"

She blinked at him, her eyes widening slightly in surprise. But the smile that quickly followed warmed him right through to his bones. "Very. More than I ever thought I'd be."

"Because of Oz?"

"Yes. Among other things." She plucked the umbrella out of his drink and leaned her elbows on the bar, twirling it in her fingers.

"Like what?"

She sighed, more relaxed and happy than he'd ever seen her. "I can't even tell you how amazing it is to be free."

"Free?"

"Free," she said, nudging him with her shoulder. "From all the Debusshere insanity. What happened with Mom and Dad earlier?"

"Nothing."

"Are you really going to try to lie to me?"

Elliot rubbed his hand over his eyes, suddenly exhausted. "I pitched them an idea for expanding the charity into a more focused foundation."

"I'm guessing they grudgingly listened and then crapped all over it."

"Something like that," he said, taking another drink.

"And Lena?"

Elliot looked up, startled. He thought about denying it. But there really wasn't any point. Cher could always tell when he was lying. "They do not approve."

"Yeah," Cher said with a sigh. "I know how that goes."

"They saw her coming out of my room."

Cher's eyebrows disappeared into her hairline. "Oh, really."

"Yeah." He gave her a sheepish smile, more embarrassed at her finding out than he had been about his parents. Then again, he cared about Cher's opinion more. "They know she was helping me on the proposal for the foundation. It makes me wonder what they would have said if she hadn't been a part of it. But it doesn't matter whose idea it was. It's a good idea, worth doing. It shouldn't matter where it came from."

"It probably doesn't. You know them. They don't like change. And they really don't like their children branching out on their own. You rocking the boat would have been enough for them to say no."

"True. But…when they came to my room, after they saw her leaving… They said the most horrible things about her. She doesn't deserve that kind of crap from anyone. Lena's smart, Cher. She's amazing."

Cher grinned. "Yes, she is."

"They'd be lucky to have someone like her on the payroll. But because she's not running in their circles, they think she's…"

Cher patted her brother's arm. "Yeah. Been there."

"Yeah. They weren't too thrilled with Oz, either," Elliot said.

"It wasn't quite as bad for us. I was on my own, in another state, working at a job that I loved and they hated. They could hate my life all they wanted. It's a lot easier to deal with from a thousand miles away."

Elliot laughed. "Yeah, I guess it would be."

"I'm doing what I love now. I've got my shop up and running. Every day I get to help women set up for being out on their own, in a good job. I'm happy. You have no idea what it's like to make a decision and not have to wonder how it will make Mom react or if you'll get that *look* from Dad. I know they love us and want the best for us, but the way they go about showing it…"

"Sucks."

Cher nodded. "Yes, it does. You can't let them keep doing it to you, Elliot. It's your life. You aren't ever going to be happy until you start living it the way you want to."

Elliot shook his head. "I don't even know where to start."

"I think you do," Cher said, smiling.

He kept his gaze firmly on his coconut. He didn't like to admit that he was afraid, but the hard knot in the pit of his stomach was a pretty strong reminder. Maybe his parents weren't the only ones who didn't like change. Change was hard.

"I don't think I could have done it without Oz," Cher said, her attention back on the twirling umbrella in her fingers.

"Done what?"

"Broken free. One thirteen hour car ride with him and

my life was changed."

"He encouraged you to get out on your own?"

Cher laughed. "Encouraged? Hell, he flat-out dared me to quit being a baby and do what I really wanted to do with my life. I'd started in the right direction, but I don't know if I ever would have gone all the way without him there with me."

Elliot nodded. "He's a great guy."

Cher looked at him, her gaze raking over his face. "Lena is a lot like him."

"Is she?"

She nodded. "I don't know what it is about those two. I wish I could have met their parents. Oz and Lena are... strong. Full of life. There's just something about them..."

Elliot pictured Lena's softly smiling face, her quiet strength, the inner beauty and goodness she exuded without even trying. "I know what you mean."

"She's something, isn't she? The first time I met her, she hugged me so tight I thought she'd crack my back." Cher laughed. "That's just how she is. I always wondered how she could have so many doubts about herself because when it comes to those she loves, she's fierce. I've never met anyone more loving and fun to be around. And the way her brain works downright scares me sometimes."

Elliot snorted. "Yeah. It was fun to watch how she can take one little nugget of a thought and turn it into this amazing idea. If she had the right resources, she could take over the world."

"Sounds like someone else I know."

"Who?"

"You."

Elliot stared at her, pride filling him that she had that kind of faith in him. Pride tinged with fear. And doubt.

"I wouldn't ever want to let them down," he said quietly, finally giving voice to the real fear that had been tearing at his gut since he realized he might want something more substantial with Lena.

"Lena and Tyler?"

Elliot nodded. "Tyler..." He laughed. "That kid is something else."

"He's pretty great, isn't he?"

"Yeah. He is. I'm glad Oz has always been there for him. He needs a good dad in his life."

"And you don't think you can be that for him?"

Elliot's hand clenched his coconut, the knot in his gut twisting tighter. "I'd like to be, I think. I want to try. But I don't know how. I guess I never really thought of myself as dad material."

"And now?"

Elliot stared into his drink for a minute, seeing flashes of Tyler's face laughing up at him, shouting for joy when he beat him at a game, resting like an angel while he slept.

Elliot looked at Cher, a smile spreading across his face.

She leaned over and kissed his cheek. "I think you've got your answer."

She stood up and slapped a couple twenties onto the bar. "The coconuts are on me. Now, I'm going to get some beauty sleep. I've got an important date tomorrow."

Elliot stood and wrapped his arms around his sister. "I love you, Cher-Bear."

"Love you, too, Smelliot. Now go get some sleep."

"Yes, ma'am."

The knot in Elliot's gut loosened a bit as he watched his sister walk away. He didn't know what the future held. He didn't know if he and Lena could make it work or not. He didn't know if he'd be able to make a foundation run without his parents' backing.

But he did know if he didn't try, he'd regret it the rest of his life.

Chapter Seventeen

"Tyler, hold still for one more second. I need to fasten your bow tie."

Tyler pouted but managed to contain himself long enough for Lena to get his tie on. She didn't blame him for being antsy. There was a palpable tension in the air as everyone got ready for the wedding. An excitement that everyone was having a hard time containing. Except for Cher's parents, of course. Then again, they were always cool as ice and would probably be thrilled if their daughter changed her mind.

The only child of theirs who didn't disappoint them was Lilah. But she hadn't been able to attend the wedding, since she had an emergency with a patient who she couldn't leave. Cher was the black sheep who was cementing that reputation by marrying Oz in a few short minutes.

And Elliot... Well, Lena wasn't sure yet where Elliot would end up standing with his parents. She'd planned to wait until after the wedding to talk to him. She wasn't sure what she'd say yet. She hoped they could work something out between them. But the morning had been a whirlwind of preparation, and she hadn't even seen him. The ladies all had their hair and makeup done at the hotel's salon and were decked out in their bridesmaid gear. Cher was absolutely stunning in a sleeveless mermaid style dress covered in soft lace. Lena had been able to catch Oz, handsome as ever in his tux, for a quick hug.

But Elliot she hadn't seen at all. She nearly trembled with the urge to go find him, throw her arms around him, and beg him to give them a chance. Only she'd try to play it a lot more cool than that. If she could. If he'd even talk to her.

She ran a quick hand over Tyler's tux, straightened his bow tie, and handed him the ring bearer pillow. The rings were safe in Oz's best man's pocket until right before the ceremony.

"There," she said, giving his tie one last tug. "You look handsome."

"I don't like this tie. No one else has to wear one."

"That's not true. Uncle Oz and all his friends are wearing them. So is…Elliot."

"Elliot is wearing one, too?"

"Yep."

Tyler thought about that for a second and then nodded his head. "Okay, then."

Lena gazed thoughtfully at her son. She didn't know how much to discuss with him. He was only six. But if Elliot was going to be a part of their lives, she needed to find out how Tyler felt about it so she'd at least have a heads-up if there were going to be issues.

"Hey, Ty," she said, squatting down so she could look into his eyes. "How do you feel about Elliot? Do you like him?"

Tyler's little face lit up. "Yeah! He's really cool. Can we visit him after we go home?"

Lena smiled at her son and grabbed him for a quick hug. "I don't know, sweetie. We'll see, okay?"

Tyler's grin filled his face, and he gave Lena two big thumbs-up.

It surprised her, since he usually assumed "we'll see" meant no. Maybe he could tell the difference in her voice… Because this time, she meant exactly what she said. She couldn't promise him anything before speaking to Elliot. But she was hopeful.

Elliot paced back and forth in the elevator, impatiently waiting for the floors to tick down to Lena's. Hopefully she hadn't left for the ceremony yet. He'd planned on waiting until after the wedding to talk to her, but he couldn't wait anymore.

New plan. He was going to find Lena and kiss her until she agreed to give them a shot. Hell, he'd beg her if he had to. Follow her to North Carolina and camp out on her lawn. Do whatever it damn well took to convince her she could count on him, that he was exactly what she and Tyler needed in their lives.

To hell with his parents. All he needed was her. And not just for the foundation, though he had no doubt that they could start a foundation without them. After all, he was the master fundraiser. He still had his connections. They'd be able to get a foundation off the ground. He just needed her, plain and simple. Her and Tyler. He knew they could make it work. And he would do anything it took until she believed it, too.

The doors dinged and slowly slid open. He pushed through before they'd finished opening all the way and hurried down the hall to where the ladies had taken over a suite of rooms. He burst in and a gaggle of women in mint green dresses turned to stare at him. Cher peered around their shoulders, her eyes wide in surprise.

The urgency spurring him on took a momentary pause while he took in the vision of loveliness that was his sister.

"Wow," he said, coming toward her.

She glanced down at her dress, fluffing it out a bit. "Do you think he'll like it?"

Elliot had to swallow past a suddenly tight throat but managed a nod. "You look so beautiful." He kissed her forehead and pulled her into a hug, being careful not to crush or smear anything.

She let him hold her for a second and then pulled away, reaching for a tissue that one of her bridesmaids held out.

"Thank you," she said, dabbing delicately under her eyes. She took a deep breath and flashed a brilliant smile at him. "Now, while I am happy you stopped by for a visit, I doubt you came crashing in here like a madman just to check up on me."

Elliot ducked his head, a little ashamed that he *hadn't* come by to check on her. She was his twin sister. He should have been thinking about her on the most important day of her life.

She laughed and patted his cheek. "It's okay, Elliot." She leaned in so only he could hear. "Tyler was getting antsy, so Lena took him to the courtyard a little early."

Elliot's gaze shot to hers, and she pulled him in for another quick hug. "Go get her."

"Yes, ma'am," he said, his nervous excitement kicking into overdrive.

He ran out of the room, not stopping until he hit the courtyard. The wedding planner, his parents, and most of the guests turned startled eyes to him. He ignored all of them, his eyes searching for Lena.

"Elliot!" Tyler came running up to him.

"Hey, little man. You look spiffy."

Tyler pulled at the vest beneath his tux jacket. "Mommy says all the men have to wear this." He looked Elliot up and down. "I look just like you!"

Elliot laughed and ruffled Tyler's hair. "Yes, you do. Very handsome."

Lena turned the corner and came to a stop when she saw him talking to Tyler.

"Hey, Tyler, do you mind if I talk to your mom for a second?"

Tyler nodded with a huge grin on his face. "You sit right here and don't go anywhere, okay?" Elliot said, plopping him onto one of the seats that had been set up for the ceremony.

He walked toward Lena, his gaze locked on hers until he stood just a breath away. They stared at each other for half a heartbeat. And then Lena was in his arms and his lips were on hers, kissing her with a desperation he'd never dreamed he'd feel. His hands moved up to cup her face. She wrapped her arms around him, kissing him as though he were the very air she needed to breathe.

There was an outraged gasp, probably from his parents, but Elliot ignored it and continued worshipping the woman in his arms until she clung to him with a quivering sigh. He finally pulled away so he could look into her eyes, tracing his thumbs across her cheeks. Lena turned her face into his hands to cuddle against him. She kissed his palm and gazed back up at him with such a look of heat and happiness that his heart almost stopped.

"Lena," he moaned, leaning his forehead against hers until he caught his breath. "God, you're beautiful."

She smiled, gentle and sweet, and he caressed her face again, forcing a breath past the nervousness running rampant through him. "I want to try and give this a shot. You and me. If you're willing." His eyes searched hers. "Do you want this? Want me?"

She gazed up at him, and he held his breath. If the way she'd kissed him was any indication, he was good to go. But just because she kissed him didn't mean she wanted anything more than that. Trying to make a relationship between them work would be tough. She might not want to risk it, especially with Tyler.

Lena reached up and stroked his cheek, then leaned forward and placed a soft kiss on his lips. "Yes."

His heart leaped, and he looked into her eyes to make sure he heard her right. "Yes? You want me?"

She kissed him again. "More than anything I've ever wanted."

He pulled her to him, kissing her hard and fast. "Good! Come on."

Elliot grabbed her hand and pulled her farther into the

courtyard.

"Elliot!" she said, laughing. "Where are we going?"

"To talk to my parents."

"Your parents?" He felt a slight resistance in her hand, but she didn't pull away from him. "Why?"

"I've got something to say to them."

Before Lena could ask any more questions, Elliot pulled her up the aisle to where his parents stood in front of the arch of foliage Cher and Oz would wed under. His mother had paused, while instructing one of the staff members to tack back some of the ribbons that trailed from the display, to stare at them in astonishment. The look intensified when he and Lena barreled up to her. His father came to stand beside his mom, his face already set in disapproving lines. Typical.

"Mom, Dad, I know you don't approve of my plans to expand the charity. But I'm going to go ahead with them, anyway. I'd like to share our plans with the rest of the board and get their input. I know you like things the way they are, but everything could be run much better, and I intend to see it done. You put me in charge of the charity, so let me truly run it. And if you and the board all vote against me, then Lena and I will start a foundation without your backing. It would be better to expand on what is already there, but this idea is good. It's worthwhile, and with Lena's brains and my contacts, I have no doubt we can make it a success."

His parents stared at him, stunned into silence for once in their lives. His dad recovered first.

"Elliot," his dad said, "we discussed this already, and we decided against it."

Elliot nodded and took a deep breath, holding on to

Lena to give him strength for the words he never thought he'd say. "Then I resign. I'll start my own foundation, without your help."

His father's face flushed bright red, and he opened his mouth to respond, but his mom put her hand on his arm.

"Now is not the time or place for this conversation."

His dad blinked and looked around at the wedding guests and staff that had begun to filter in and were now watching the confrontation.

"Actually, now is the perfect time," Elliot said. "I've spent my whole life waiting for something amazing to come along. Well, something finally has," he said, drawing Lena closer to him. "I'm not going to let her get away." He turned back to his parents. "And I'm not going to let this idea go, either. I'm going to create this foundation, with Lena at my side."

His mother looked at him, a thoughtful expression on her face. But his father stepped closer, as near to truly losing his temper as Elliot had ever seen him.

"You're going to go against us? For her?"

Elliot's blood pressure shot up until he could feel the vein throbbing in his neck. He really hadn't wanted to make this a drag-out fight, but if his father didn't watch what he said about Lena, things were going to get ugly fast.

His father continued on as if he wasn't aware that Elliot was almost at his breaking point. He probably didn't. He hadn't ever paid attention to what Elliot felt.

"You've spent your whole life working to get where you're at now. Think long and hard about what you are throwing away before you do this, Son."

Elliot shook his head. "Throw away? I'm not throwing

anything away, Dad. I'm gaining more than I ever dreamed possible. This incredible woman is willing to stand by my side and help me make something worthwhile out of my life. How many people ever find someone like that? She's brave and brilliant and the most beautiful person, inside and out, that I've ever had the pleasure to know. I'm not throwing anything away for the chance to be with her. I'm giving myself the opportunity to achieve everything I ever wanted. She's amazing. And so is her son. I'm falling for both of them, and the only tragedy here would be if I threw away the chance to see what the three of us can become."

His parents were struck well and truly speechless. It was probably the best moment of Elliot's life.

Then Lena started to laugh. He turned to her, eyebrows raised. His parents stared at her like she'd gone crazy. Maybe she had… It *had* been kind of an intense morning so far.

"Sorry," she gasped, cupping his face and giving him a quick kiss while her shoulders still shook with laughter. "I was so nervous about what I was going to say to convince you to give us, and your foundation, a chance. And you just said everything that I had been thinking. We are on the exact same page. Again," she said, beaming up at him.

He laughed with her, his heart soaring. "Well, I guess that answers the rest of my questions."

He drew her in against him.

"Elliot, this conversation is not over," his dad said.

Elliot didn't even look at them. He kept his gaze firmly glued to Lena's. "Yes, Dad. It is."

Then he leaned down and kissed the woman in his arms, letting his lips show her how much he'd come to value her, how excited he was to discover their future together, how much he wanted to take her back to his room and show her everything he was feeling in a little more detail. Okay, a lot more detail.

The wedding guests erupted in applause, clapping and cheering until Elliot and Lena looked up, startled. Lena laughed and tucked her head against Elliot's neck, hiding a little from the audience they had apparently accumulated. Oz and Cher whooped loudly from the back of the courtyard.

"Shit," Elliot said quietly so only Lena could hear him. "I think we just upstaged the bride and groom."

Lena glanced back at their beaming siblings. "I don't think they mind."

"All right, all right!" Oz called. "I'm glad you two have finally come to your senses. But can we get on with our wedding now? My honeymoon starts in four hours, and we've got a flight on a puddle jumper to the next island. We don't want to miss it!"

Everyone laughed and Elliot took a little bow, then escorted Lena back to the staging area where they got in line with the other wedding attendants. They marched up the aisle together, stood smiling at each while Oz and Cher said their vows, and cheered louder than anyone else when the pastor pronounced them Mr. and Mrs. Nathaniel Oserkowski.

On the way back down the aisle, Tyler ran over to them, and Elliot scooped him up in one arm and wrapped the other around Lena's waist. Caught between the two of them, Elliot thought it was safe to say he'd never been so happy in his entire life.

And it was just the beginning.

Epilogue

Lena stood at the edge of the pool at Elliot's North Carolina house, staring down into the clear water with her heart pounding in her throat. Elliot and Tyler had been splashing around for fifteen minutes already, but so far, they hadn't been able to coax her in. She'd gotten over her fears enough that she could wade into the shallow end and relax enough for it to be enjoyable, but that was in the shallow end, and only if she could take her time getting in. Elliot wanted her to jump. All the way in. All at once. Into the deep end. He had dared her to. She couldn't ignore a straight-out dare. But she wasn't sure she could man-up and jump in, either.

She sucked in several deep breaths. She wasn't sure, but it was a good bet that she was on the verge of hyperventilating. It didn't help that his pool was three-times the size of the pool at her condo complex. When she'd finally been able to save enough money, thanks to what she made working for the foundation and from her gift basket and all-natural remedy sales, she and Tyler had gotten their own place. Getting one with a pool had been Elliot's idea. One she'd liked and had even learned to enjoy. It was big enough to play in but not enough to give her a total panic attack. Not anymore. Elliot had been working with her. Their tub sessions were… She shivered with remembered pleasure, wishing she was back in his big garden bathtub right then instead of staring at the wrong end of several thousand gallons of water.

Elliot's tub she'd take any day. But his pool… She wasn't sure she was ready for that yet.

"Come on, Len. I'll catch you." Elliot reached his arms out to her.

For a moment, she forgot to be terrified. Staring at the wet and naked chest of the firmly muscled and gorgeous man that she'd just spent the night worshiping had that effect on her.

Elliot's gaze turned smoldering, fully aware what she was thinking.

"Come on," he said again. "You jump in, and I'll give you an extra special reward tonight."

Water trickled down his chest, following the grooves and ridges of his muscles. Lena's mouth went a little dry. She swallowed, her fears almost totally eclipsed by thoughts of a much more naughty nature.

He held his arms out to her again. Lena took a deep breath, letting go of all her fears. He'd catch her; she had no doubt of that. She trusted him. Implicitly. And not just because of the ring he'd put on her finger the night before in the living room of her new place.

Tyler squealed. "Yay! Can we sleep over, Mommy?"

Lena smiled, her eyes focused on Elliot. And the future they'd planned for their new family.

She jumped, knowing he'd always be there to catch her.

Author's Note

In this book, Elliot's foundation, KidsCase, is modeled on a real organization based out of Tracy, California called Case For Kids. Case for Kids is a nonprofit agency that donates personalized cases to children in foster care. These custom cases are decorated with each child's first name and are packed with new clothes, a homemade blanket, a sheet set, toiletries, a stuffed animal, and a book.

The mission of Case for Kids is to improve a child's self-esteem by replacing garbage bags as their form of luggage with a personalized bin to be used when relocating from foster care agencies into foster care homes. So many times these children come into the system with nothing to call their own. Case for Kids is doing what it can to help.

To find out how you can help or for more information on this wonderful organization, please visit their website or Facebook page.

http://caseforkids.org/
https://www.facebook.com/CaseForKids

Acknowledgments

First of all, to my readers—I wouldn't be here without you and being able to share my stories with you is very truly a dream come true. Thank you so much for all your support!

To my amazing editors Erin Molta, Heather Howland, and Curtis Svehlak. I don't know how you guys do it but your fabulousness knows no bounds. I am thrilled to get to work with you. Thank you so much for all you do.

To Sarah—DITTO! So very much ditto. Ha! You didn't think I'd say it. All the feels, woman. All the feels. I'd crumble without your support. Or at least be completely off my rocker, and we both know what a short trip that would be.

To my amazing husband—this job would be difficult, if not downright impossible, without your support. Thank you for putting up with my crazy deadline personality, my late nights and early mornings, and "oops I forgot to get dressed today" moments. Thank you for keeping the kids fed and entertained and for working so hard to make sure my dreams could come true. Love you, babe. Kids—your goofiness and smiling little faces make my world go 'round. Jeanette—I'm beyond blessed to have a sister as a best friend. Thank you for always being there. You're incredible, lady. You inspire me every day.

About the Author

Kira Archer resides in Pennsylvania with her husband, two kiddos, and far too many animals in the house. She tends to laugh at inappropriate moments, break all the rules she gives her kids (but only when they aren't looking), and would rather be reading a book than doing almost anything else. She has odd, eclectic tastes in just about everything and often lets her imagination run away with her. She loves a vast variety of genres and writes in quite a few. If you love historical romances, check out her alter ego, Michelle McLean.

DRIVING HER CRAZY

Cher Debusshere hates being the black sheep of her posh family as much as she hates driving. When her flight to her sister's wedding is grounded (*fan-freakin'-tastic*), oh-so-sexy Nathaniel "Oz" Oserkowski offers to share both the car rental *and* the driving duties. Now he's just driving her crazy by assuming Cher's some spoiled little rich girl. But as they bait and needle each other, their lust and longing is hot enough to overheat the engine. They have nothing in common…but sometimes it takes a journey to change the destination.

Made in the USA
Las Vegas, NV
31 July 2022